British Terrorist Novels of the 1970s

Joseph Darlington

British Terrorist Novels of the 1970s

Joseph Darlington
Futureworks Media School
Manchester, UK

ISBN 978-3-030-08567-4   ISBN 978-3-319-77896-9 (eBook)
https://doi.org/10.1007/978-3-319-77896-9

© The Editor(s) (if applicable) and The Author(s) 2018
Softcover re-print of the Hardcover 1st edition 2018
This work is subject to copyright. All rights are solely and exclusively licensed by the Publisher, whether the whole or part of the material is concerned, specifically the rights of translation, reprinting, reuse of illustrations, recitation, broadcasting, reproduction on microfilms or in any other physical way, and transmission or information storage and retrieval, electronic adaptation, computer software, or by similar or dissimilar methodology now known or hereafter developed.
The use of general descriptive names, registered names, trademarks, service marks, etc. in this publication does not imply, even in the absence of a specific statement, that such names are exempt from the relevant protective laws and regulations and therefore free for general use.
The publisher, the authors and the editors are safe to assume that the advice and information in this book are believed to be true and accurate at the date of publication. Neither the publisher nor the authors or the editors give a warranty, express or implied, with respect to the material contained herein or for any errors or omissions that may have been made. The publisher remains neutral with regard to jurisdictional claims in published maps and institutional affiliations.

Cover design: Fatima Jamadar

Printed on acid-free paper

This Palgrave Macmillan imprint is published by the registered company Springer International Publishing AG part of Springer Nature
The registered company address is: Gewerbestrasse 11, 6330 Cham, Switzerland

Contents

1 Introduction 1

2 A Short History of Terrorism as Concept and Tactic 9

3 The Terrorist Novel, Thrillers and Postcolonial Britain 33

4 Writing the IRA from the Mainland: Truth and Fiction 59

5 Countercultural Writers and The Angry Brigade 87

6 Environmentalists and Conservationists: Terrorising the Countryside 117

7 Conclusion 143

Index 151

CHAPTER 1

Introduction

During the writing of this book the popular conception of international terrorism has changed shape at least twice. I first noticed the preponderance of 1970s terror novels back in 2010. Al Qaida was then the face of international terror. Nine years on from the World Trade Centre attacks their enigmatic leader Osama bin Laden was still at large and, in the mind of the average British person, a "terrorist attack" meant a bombing conducted by an organised cell of committed jihadis. Four years later I was completing my Ph.D. on a different but related set of mid-century novelists, bin Laden was dead, and Al Qaida's place in the media spotlight had been overtaken by the new terror threat, the Islamic State. ISIS turned away from the cultivation of international networks and instead focused on building a really existing Caliphate among the war-torn wreckage of Iraq and Syria. Suddenly, it appeared there was a whole country of terrorists. The British media was no longer obsessed with foreign terrorists entering Britain, but with British-born youths turning jihadi and flying over to join the insurrection. As I sit here typing now, in 2017, the terrible carnage in the Middle East has resulted in a refugee crisis to match that of the Second World War. European governments have opened their doors to these migrants, with Germany and Sweden leading by example. The British government's efforts, by comparison, have been comparatively meagre. This is largely attributable to the new vehicular form of terrorist attack first carried out in Nice in July 2016, then in Berlin in December 2016 and, most recently, in London and Stockholm in 2017. Gone are the days of elaborate networks of underground terrorist cells. When the average British person thinks of a terrorist attack in 2017, they think of a lone attacker whose only weapons are trucks and kitchen knives but who, perhaps because of this very lack of sophistication, prove totally unpredictable.

This book does not aim to provide any answers regarding contemporary terrorism. I begin with these statements merely to indicate the extent to which our understanding of terrorism can shift within the stretch of only a few short years. And this is only the most prominent narrative around terrorism; the picture becomes even less clear when we introduce far right terrorists, Boko Haram, The Invisible Committee, Hamas, or cyber-terrorism involving a huge range of disparate groups from LulzSec to the Russian state. Terrorism is a complex thing, and it's often said that one man's terrorist is another man's freedom fighter. Some things are, however, definitely terrorism. These problems don't go away when we put quotation marks around them. It is for that reason that I have refused to opt for the distancing form—"terrorism"—favoured by many academics. I trust that you, as readers of an academic monograph, will be capable of detecting ambiguities of usage yourselves without my foregrounding them. Indeed, the core of this book's argument is that it is the very flexibility of the concept, terrorism, which makes it valuable as a tool for historical analysis. The ways in which British society has used the word terrorism have shifted not only in response to the real-life terrorist threats that it faces, but also in relation to the way it perceives itself, the lines it draws between liberty and security, and the level of tolerance which it holds for radical ideas. The 1970s are the setting for this study, and British novels are its subject matter. You will find that the ways they deal with terrorism are often alien to our contemporary mores, and yet, in context, they are always comprehensible. If this shifts your perceptions of terrorism then so be it. It is not the primary purpose of this text.

This study came about due to a separate study related to experimental writing in Britain during the 1970s. The decade's politics were perhaps best described by Francis Wheen as a "pungent melange of apocalyptic dread and conspiratorial fever" (2010, 9). In order to better immerse myself in the structures of feeling predominating at this time I took to reading pulpy thriller novels (this also provided a much-needed respite from the complex, avant-garde material I was *supposed* to be reading).

As I worked my way down the Corgi bestseller lists and into the lesser-known paperbacks, I noticed a recurring trope, jarring at first but eventually becoming an obsession. There were an awful lot of novels published in Britain in the 1970s in which terrorists were the main protagonists. Initially, I thought this may have been a trend common in the thriller genre overall which I had never noticed, never being an enthusiastic reader of thrillers before this point. Research confirmed its particularity to the 1970s, however; both my own and in papers like Appelbaum and Paknadel's longitudinal study. Alex Houen's groundbreaking book, *Terrorism and Literature* (2001), demonstrates that literature encounters terrorism throughout the twentieth century, but it makes no comment on the quantity of works published. Randall, Banita and Rothberg, among others, have commented on the glut of terror-themed novels published post-2001, although the number with terrorist protagonists remained low. Discussing my initial research at the International Terrorism and Aesthetics conference in Szeged, Hungary, in 2011, I was confirmed in my suspicions that this was an important, under-researched phenomenon. The work then continued for another six years, trying to make sense of this initial finding. What I found is as follows.

In order to understand both the novel and perceptions of terrorism in any given society, one must embed them in the historical conditions from which they are produced. Terrorism has its own history, as both a concept and a tactic, which must be addressed first in order to grasp its importance in a given moment. The reasoning behind any given act of terror can be manifold and often opaque, but the form of action we define as terrorism is one that is shaped by preceding acts. Terrorism changes but it is not reinvented anew on each occasion. The history of terrorism framing the 1970s novels which are this study's main concern is outlined in Chapter 2. Drawing on the work of terrorism and security studies, this chapter argues that terrorism as a concept emerges alongside the development of the nation state. Assassins and zealots precede this historical juncture, but it is only with the formal elevation of the body politic to the basis of constitutional power that terror as an explicitly *political* force can be seen to exist. From this point, Chapter 2 traces terrorism's troubled relationship to anarchism, National Socialism and Marxism, before it was eventually translated into the guerrilla doctrine and its doomed 1970s sibling—the urban guerrilla. The chapter closes with an overview of the standard terrorist novel narrative.

This morphology emerged in response to repeated tropes in terrorist fiction and the majority of novels covered in this study conform to it, more or less. Like all structures it is contingent, but it is important to establish before moving on to the content of the novels themselves.

Chapters 3–6 focus on distinct categories of terrorism encountered in 1970s novels. Some, like Chapter 5, engage with one particular group's impact; others, like Chapter 3, ask broader questions about how these novels relate to British identity in the 1970s. For ease of reference I have also listed here the key texts engaged with in each chapter in the hope this makes the work more navigable for reference purposes.

THE TERRORIST NOVEL, THRILLERS AND POSTCOLONIAL BRITAIN

Chapter 3 places the British terror novel in both its national and international context. Although the end of Empire had been feted since the 1950s (Whittle 2016, 14), the 1970s saw a renewed postcolonial funk dominating Britain's understanding of its role in the world. The 1973 recession which marks the decade's break from 1960s prosperity is largely blamed on the Oil Crisis; an embargo by Arab states on trading with the West. Common depictions of foreign terrorists conform to colonial prejudices regarding race but are also contrasted against depictions of Britain and its agents as powerless in a postcolonial world. By analysing postcolonial structures of feeling, this chapter also establishes the core themes which will emerge throughout the proceeding study including questions of belief, authenticity and commitment, the morality of violence, and role of the state in the protection of liberty. From a primarily foreign focus, the chapter then goes on to show how Britain itself is presented in a postcolonial manner. Terrorist novels written from left, right and centrist perspectives all consider the meaning of Britain following the collapse of its Empire and the foundation of multiculturalism.

Key texts: *The Honorary Consul* (Graham Greene 1973), *Guerrillas* (V.S. Naipaul 1975), *The Levanter* (Eric Ambler 1972), *The Day of the Jackal* (Fredrick Forsyth 1971), *The Volunteers* (Raymond Williams 1978), *Who Killed Enoch Powell?* (Arthur Wise 1970), *The Chilian Club* (George Shipway 1971).

WRITING THE IRA FROM THE MAINLAND: TRUTH AND FICTION

Chapter 4 focuses on the number-one terrorist threat to Britain during the 1970s—the Provisional IRA—and the correspondingly few terrorist novels which feature them. Drawing on the large and detailed body of scholarship now existing relating to the conflict in Northern Ireland, this chapter focuses on investigating the truths and falsehoods about the IRA which are communicated in the novels. By comparing fact to fiction, the content of the novels, many of them bestsellers, reveal the processes of miscommunication and misunderstanding through which the conflict was mediated to the British public. The chapter then extends its analysis of popular misinformation to investigate Claire Sterling's claims that the Provisional IRA was part of an international terror network directed and funded by the Soviet Union.

Key texts: *Harry's Game* (Gerald Seymour 1975) and *The Glory Boys* (Gerald Seymour 1976), *The Family Arsenal* (Paul Theroux 1976), *The Sweets of Pimlico* (A.N. Wilson 1977), *The Good Terrorist* (Doris Lessing 1985).

COUNTERCULTURAL WRITERS AND THE ANGRY BRIGADE

Chapter 5 concerns the left-wing terrorist group The Angry Brigade (shambolic counterpart to the Italian Red Brigades and German Red Army Faction) and the surprising level of sympathy these terrorists drew from the broader British left. This chapter takes a biographical approach to the subject matter, tracing connections between The Angry Brigade and the writers of terrorist novels themselves. It investigates how this perceived closeness between writer and bomber impacts these novelists' work and connects them to trends within the counterculture overall. The networks of sympathisers allow urban guerrilla theorising to infiltrate left-wing theory during this era such that it still holds influence today.

Key texts: *Snipe's Spinster* (Jeff Nuttall 1975), *Magnificence* (Howard Brenton 1973), *The Angry Brigade* (Alan Burns 1973), *Christie Malry's Own Double-Entry* (B.S. Johnson 1973), *The Infernal Desire Machines of Doctor Hoffman* (Angela Carter 1972), *Esther, Ruth and Jennifer* (Jack Davies 1979).

Environmentalists and Conservationists: Terrorising the Countryside

Chapter 6 moves from political concerns to broadly environmentalist concerns. It describes the historical convergence of progressive environmentalist groups with conservative conservationist groups that occurred early in the decade and how this split is embodied in two very different types of terrorist novel. The first, championing animal rights and ecology as its core concerns, is largely written for an urban, left-wing audience and can be seen to lay the theoretical groundwork for the eco-terrorist of the 1990s. As there exists no quintessential novel of this type published in Britain at this time, the chapter begins instead with an analysis of American bestseller *The Monkey Wrench Gang*. British novels of the 1970s which integrate eco-terrorists into their narratives are studied in relation to this inspirational urtext. The second type of terrorist novel centres on the country house as a symbol of British rural conservation at threat from municipal planning authorities. Largely satirical, the aristocratic terrorist heroes of these texts raise questions about the pleasurable potential of fictional terrorism. Terrorist heroes are then seen to provide catharsis for traditionalists tired of the welfare state.

Key texts: *The Monkey Wrench Gang* (Edward Abbey 1975), *I Want to Go to Moscow* (Maureen Duffy 1973), *The Dynostar Menace* (Kit Pedler and Gerry Davis 1976), *The Adventures of Una Persson and Catherine Cornelius in the 20th Century* (Michael Moorcock 1976), *Blott on the Landscape* (Tom Sharpe 1975), *Last of the Country House Murders* (Emma Tennant 1974).

The book then concludes by considering the resurgence of the 1970s terrorist narratives in the years following 9/11. It is suggested that although there appears to be very little interest in creating sympathetic terrorist protagonists in fiction set in the contemporary moment, the exploration of these ideas is taking place in contemporary historical fiction. The 1970s in these post-2001 texts represents a safe, but still relevant distance in which the unsayable may still be said.

The shifts in terrorist threat, and our attitudes to them, is finally considered in relation to Anthony Burgess' *1985* (1978).

Bibliography

Appelbaum, Robert, and Alexis Paknadel. 2008. Terrorism and the Novel, 1970–2001. *Poetics Today* 29 (3): 387–436.

Banita, Georgia. 2012. *Plotting Justice: Narrative Ethics and Literary Culture After 9/11*. Lincoln: University of Nebraska Press.
Houen, Alex. 2001. *Terrorism and Literature*. Oxford: Oxford University Press.
Randall, Martin. 2011. *9/11 and the Literature of Terror*. Edinburgh: Edinburgh University Press.
Rothberg, Michael. 2009. A Failure of the Imagination: Diagnosing the Post-9/11 Novel. *American Literary History* 21 (1): 152–158.
Wheen, Francis. 2010. *Strange Days Indeed*. London: Fourth Estate.
Whittle, Matthew. 2016. *Post-war British Literature and the "End of Empire"*. London: Palgrave Macmillan.

CHAPTER 2

A Short History of Terrorism as Concept and Tactic

Terrorism is a word often used but rarely explained. One man's terrorist is another's freedom fighter, or so the old saying goes. But in the contemporary moment the term has also come to define an absolute, something beyond existing definitions of good and evil, legal and illegal. Where terrorists of an older generation like Nelson Mandela, Che Guevara or the Dalai Lama have gone on to attain high status among the world's moral elite, it is unlikely that any post-2001 proponent of political violence will find such a redemption narrative possible. The terrorist, like the terror laws which define them, now exist as a negation of a negation. Terrorists are not criminals. They are not found guilty by courts of law. Their existence is beyond law; it is extrajudicial, as is their torture and their death. Terrorists are also no longer just individuals and groups. There are terrorist ideologies, terrorist armies and entire terrorist nations. Terrorists commit atrocities and these atrocities are called terror. At the time of writing this, the Western alliance has been at war with terror for 15 years.

It has not always been this way, however. And although this book primarily regards only a relatively small part of terrorist history, Britain in the 1970s, establishing some kind of longer chronology is essential if we are to understand the differences between the terrorist then and the terrorist now. The weaknesses of many post-2001 analyses of terrorism stem from a lack of this historical grounding. The poverty of post-structuralism has reduced academic response to an analysis of affects; the semiotics of the bomb, mediatised trauma, and eschatological metanarratives have predominated in critical readings. Concentration upon affects leaves the dark heart of the terrorist concept untouched, exempt and philosophically extrajudicial. What is forgotten is that, ultimately, terrorism is a tactic. It is not an end in itself. It is not a singular event. It is an action undertaken with larger objectives in mind. Conceding this fact means that, in order to address terrorism at all, one must address it within the wider structural arrangement of which it is a part. A history of terrorism will, therefore, show very little beyond the fluidity of terrorism as a concept. No one definition will emerge, nor even a shared set of techniques or sense of ideological extremity. As with any history of a keyword, it is ultimately an invitation to consider language as historically situated and, in the case of terrorism, politically situated as well.

Alex Houen, in his groundbreaking 2001 work *Terrorism and Modern Literature*, directs the reader's attention to one of the most common tropes in historical terrorology; the contention that "the practice of terror is an ancient one – assassination, for example, being a favourite tactic of the *Sicarii* in Palestine… and of the *Hashashin* in Persia" (2001, 19). One might also include here medieval poisoners or Japanese ninja as early practitioners of politically inspired killing. These actions certainly appear to conform to contemporary ideas of terrorism as murderous and surreptitious, dramatic in its action and intended to produce calamitous effects upon the society it targets. However, there is a key element missing which is at the core of most contemporary definitions: targeting civilians. Jonathan Barker, for example, argues for:

> A simple and straight definition that corresponds to the idea of terrorism that most people hold. It has three elements: violence threatened or employed; against civilian targets; for political objectives… unlike many other definitions, this one applied to governments (and their agencies and proxies) as well as to non-governmental groups and individuals. (2003, 23–24)

Regardless of who assassins targeted, the concept of a civilian is itself an anachronism when addressing the pre-modern world. Civilians belong to the era of constitutional states and legitimate armies. The tactics of Vlad the Impaler may be horrific, and the massacres perpetrated by the Inquisition may terrify, but they are unbounded by a legal system which separates combatant and non-combatant, legitimate and illegitimate warfare. As such they are not terrorism as we understand it. The prehistory of terrorism can help us to establish what terrorism *feels* like, but it sheds no light on the modern phenomenon from a definitional perspective. The conceptualisation of terror is bound up with the formation of the nation state and, in particular, the constitutional forms which nation states took during the era of republican revolutions.

It is in the framing of the first republican government, following the French Revolution, where terrorism first emerges as a political term. The rise of the Jacobins and the era known as the Terror peaked with Robespierre's infamous proclamation on the principles of public morality—arguably the first terrorist manifesto:

> If the mainspring of popular government in peacetime is virtue, the mainspring of popular government in revolution is virtue and terror both: virtue, without which terror is disastrous; terror, without which virtue is powerless. Terror is nothing but prompt, severe, inflexible justice; it is therefore an emanation of virtue. (2007a, 115)

Terrorism, the use of violence in pursuit of political aims, is notably initiated *by* the state rather than against it. It is not a virtue taken to an extreme, it is—in Robespierre's framing at least—simply the functional enactment of political virtue. It is the power that brings powerless virtue into the world. Importantly, this framing also raises terror above the level of brute violence to a conceptual category in itself. The guillotine was not simply a humane scientific improvement upon the nooses and axes of the *ancien régime*, it represented a new, systematic approach to law. Terror was not a punishment but a guarantor. It is the bringing of virtue into the world. As Robespierre phrased it in 1793, "the laws of eternal justice used to be called, disdainfully, the dreams of well-meaning people; we have turned them into imposing realities" (2007b, 93). Although this vision was hardly shared by anyone outside of the hardline Jacobins, there is undoubtedly a kernel of truth in Robespierre's theories about violence's role in state formation. In order to translate from mere proclamations to actual rules and regulation, the law must impose itself upon the body politic through actants. Where a developed state has its apparatuses, ideological and bureaucratic as much as repressive, at its revolutionary emergence in the eighteenth century the state inherited the precedence of violence.

If the French Revolution presented the world with its first terrorists then Edmund Burke's *Reflections on the Revolution in France* represent the first conceptual development of anti-terrorism as a coherent political position. Burke viewed the French Revolution from the start as a "monstrous tragic-comic scene [with] alternate contempt and indignation; alternate laughter and tears; alternate scorn and horror" (1986, 92–93). The "wild litigious spirit" of republicanism was anathema to "the rights of Englishmen [which are] a patrimony derived from their forefathers" (1986, 118). The natural state of society, for Burke, was one defined by heritage, lineage, gradualism and compromise. The chief enemy of society is reason which, incapable of compromise and totalising in its vision, would lead inevitably to conflict and terror. Burke's earlier aesthetic judgment that "whatever is qualified to cause terror, is a foundation capable of the sublime" (2008, 119) will be unpacked later on in this study. As an example of British moderation against French terrorism, however, it is sufficient for us now to note how this early rendering of extremism as a political category bears little resemblance to contemporary anti-extremism narratives propounded by the state. It is in fact historically opposed to the very constitutional foundation of that state. Terror is the emergence of ideological consciousness onto the stage of history. Where Burke sees government as an organic residue of the world as it is, terror aims to align the world to the terrorist's vision of it.

A century passes before terrorism rises again as a political force. The turn of the twentieth century sees a range of terrorist groups emerging on the political fringes. In Britain, these included the anarchist and Fenian bombers in London who inspired Conrad's *The Secret Agent* (1907) and Chesterton's *The Man Who Was Thursday* (1907). Their tactics bridged the space between dissent to win concessions and dissent as pure antagonism. Somewhere between these two positions fell the revolutionary theory of Louis Auguste Blanqui, whose disillusion following the failure of the Paris Commune led him to reconceive of revolution as the business of a small cadre of intellectuals. This vanguard, unlike the unpredictable masses, could assume power and establish a dictatorship. The dictatorship could then act on behalf of the people without worrying about the messy business of democracy. Blanquism, although vigorously denied by most terrorist groupings as elitist, undoubtedly represents the core of terrorist tactics from this point onwards. Orlandrew E. Danzell summarised this tendency in terms of "terrorism… perpetrated by elites. In most cases, it represents the displeasure of a fragment of the elite toward a political system, who may take it upon themselves to act on the behalf of a majority unaware of their plight" (2011, 89).

Sometimes these elites imagined themselves to be "waking up" the unaware majority through their actions, inspiring them to revolution as a result. Sometimes, as with the nihilists, their actions aimed at instigating the destruction of the existing system, leaving the unaware majority no choice but revolution after their livelihoods had been destroyed. In every case, political terror was transformed from a state policy to the act of an individual or group of individuals and, more specifically, the acts set in motion by these individuals' wills. Terrorism becomes aligned with the individual's capacity to change the world. It is a tactic that aims to impose the individual will upon society at large, upon history.

Some of the most notable terrorists to engage in these individual actions at the turn of the century were the Russian nihilists. In Russia the dizzyingly modern political theories emerging from anarchism met with the dreams of spiritual millenarians. A desire for the individual will to impose itself on history through violence wedded easily with a transcendent sense of forces acting upon the world through the medium of enlightened men. Dostoyevsky condemned this movement during its early years in *Demons* (1871/2), but it lives on in revolutionary infamy for the actions of Alexander Ulyanov. Ulyanov was executed in 1881 for murders committed as part of the group Narodnaya Volya (People's Will). "Since the current lack of political freedom meant that a mass movement was not yet possible," the group's argument went, "the only way forward was for a 'handful of daring people' to force the autocratic government to make the necessary concessions" (Lih 2011, 28–29). Bombings and political slayings were simultaneously figured as manifestations of the people's will while also, less convincingly, representing moves in a negotiation over constitutional freedoms.

Alexander Ulyanov's death shifted the historical fate of terrorism not through his own actions but by its influence upon his brother, Ilyich. Under his *nom de guerre*, Vladimir Lenin, Ilyich Ulyanov would be a central figure in the transformation of the Blanquist vanguard into a functional model for Marxist-Leninist political parties. Rather than building an underground network which emerges upon the political scene through violent actions, the Marxist-Leninist party emphasises the role of legitimate forms—elected officials, trade unions, newspapers, agitators—as drivers of popular revolt and leaders within mass movements. The underground then coordinates the public-facing bodies and, if necessary, manipulates them. The terrorist will that Blanqui celebrated is channelled instead into non-violent political channels, albeit with violent revolution as a longer term objective. It was under these conditions that Lenin could go on to reunite vanguardist terror with state terror in the dictatorship of the proletariat. Lenin's theory of the state (and of its withering away) is clearly indebted to Robespierre's use of terror to bring about virtue:

> Since the majority of the people itself suppresses its oppressors, a 'special force' for suppression is no longer necessary. In this sense the state begins to wither away.... From the state as a 'special force' for the suppression of a given class to the suppression of the oppressors by the general force of the majority of the people. (1986, 310–302)

The Marxist-Leninist party on a tactical level can therefore be seen as a bridge between terrorisms, or "political violences" if we were to treat it in the same way as other revolutionary ideologies. After all, the role of groups like the Freemasons and the Sons of Liberty in the founding of the United States bear a certain resemblance to this process, and the bloodshed which made modern America is not free of ideological fanaticisms. In addressing the Marxist-Leninist party in relation to the history of terrorism as a concept, however, it is clear that the Hobbesian attitude which permeates terrorist theory—that political conflict in the last analysis is violent conflict—is everywhere visible in its dialectical constructions. That the Bolsheviks channelled insurrectionary will into organised forms is both its triumph and its tragedy. Anarchist terrorism was rendered futile by contrast, bringing bombing campaigns across Europe and the US to an end. The rise of Bolshevism may have sublimated left-wing energies, but at the same time it pulled back the covers on political violence (to use a Burkean phrase) and made a virtue of cynicism regarding its use. Stalinist terror was not divinely inspired; it was an all too logical result of political reasoning.

By the end of the 1920s, capitalism itself appeared to collapse and brought political crisis to Europe. Right-wing nationalist vanguards arose in tandem with left-wing socialist movements and political violence became a staple of social conflict. During this period the dividing line between direct action and terrorism can only really be seen in retrospect, and any differentiation would appear arbitrary. The ideology of groups like the Black Hand, whose assassination of Franz Ferdinand provided the catalyst for the First World War, re-emerged after the war in the proto-fascist Friekorps and Romanian Iron Guard. The anarchist

George Sorel, whose 1906 *Reflections on Violence* split hairs between oppressive force and beneficial violence—"the object of *force* is to impose a certain social order in which the minority governs, while *violence* tends to the destruction of that order" (2004, 171)—was a noted inspiration for Mussolini and the Italian fascists. Philosophies of political violence transitioned from left to right, with vanguards acting on behalf of the *narod* on the one hand and *der Volk* on the other. "There is no reason to doubt the idealistic inspiration of these terrorists and their willingness if need be to sacrifice their lives," Walter Laqueur describes, "but it became abundantly clear [during this period] that terrorism was by no means a [purely] left-wing or progressive phenomenon" (1975, 13). It is here where terrorism takes on its tabloid connotations, with fascists, anarchists and communists using the label against each other while the struggling state infrastructure used it to describe all of them. It remained a label, however, rather than a specific crime, and prior to the Second World War it is just another example of the violence which marred the entire political landscape. During the war many of these groups would go on to become actors of the state, heroes of the resistance, or else be exterminated in the camps. It is only after the war ends and some form of stability returns that we can truly begin to talk again of terrorist groups in the modern sense. Terrorism, after all, is a peacetime affair. In war it's called sabotage: a more respectable tactic.

The post-war world saw a return to stability through consensus government. The experience of wartime planning and the call to support veterans of the conflict were arguably the driving factors behind the American GI Bill, and the rise of welfare states across Europe. In capitalist states, stability and normality could once again become synonymous in domestic politics. The same could not be said for the colonised nations, however, whose huge contributions to the war effort were not rewarded in anywhere like the same manner. National liberation movements gained popularity in response to this perceived injustice, turning into mass movements in the Indian subcontinent, Kenya, Uganda and Southern Rhodesia (now Zimbabwe). Where mass movements failed to gain traction, however, the temptations of the heroic vanguard arose and, with them, the adoption of terrorism. Terrorism, it was believed, could force often intractable situations in favour of the colonised. In terms of the British Empire, General Grivas in Cyprus fought a successful campaign of guerrilla warfare and urban terror using tactics perfected against the Nazis only a few years earlier. In Mandatory Palestine (now Israel and Palestine) bombing campaigns also rushed the British out of a delicate situation (the speed of which precipitated conflicts which still continue today). The French conflict in Algeria grew to such a scale that, by the early 1960s, it had spread to the metropole itself. In each of these situations the justification for terror was the same; to make the colonisers feel that the colony was no longer worth the sacrifices required to control it. In the case of the British Empire this technique was undeniably effective and may be in part responsible for the underlying malaise associated with the end of Empire. As shall be discussed later, the association of the end of Empire with terrorism accounts for the pessimistic tone of postcolonial writers like Graham Greene and V.S. Naipaul. Their writings give a sense not of a transfer of power between sovereignties, but of the once meaningful British Empire withdrawing from a world which is everywhere slipping into chaos and disorder.

The two post-war figures which come to represent the armed anti-imperialist struggle are Ernesto "Che" Guevara and Mao Tse-tung. Like Lenin a generation earlier, these figures managed to unite the vanguardist principle derived from Blanqui with the mass politics of the era. Where Lenin focused upon the urban proletariat, however, Mao and Guevara's theories of revolution focused on the rural peasantry, and where Lenin's vanguard resembled a secret society, Mao and Guevara's vanguards took the form of guerrilla combat units. Describing the "huge literature on guerrilla and counter-guerrilla warfare published in the 1950s and 1960s", Walter Laqueur is right to remind us that guerrilla warfare "has, in fact, existed for a very long time [and] predated warfare between regular armies" (2003, 341). However, the Marxist-Leninist framing of the guerrilla as merely an active representative of an unaware (but always supportive) majority was of huge importance. Firstly, it allowed Mao to portray his vanguard in terms which almost entirely dissolved its vanguardism: "the [people] may be likened to water and the [guerrilla] to the fish who inhabit it. How may it be said that these two cannot exist together?" (2007, 93). Furthermore, it allowed Guevarism to renounce terrorism as an individualist phenomenon separate and distinct from violence (sabotage) enacted by the *foco*: "sabotage has nothing to do with terrorism; terrorism and personal assaults are entirely different tactics… terrorism is negative, and in no way does it produce the desired effects" (2009, 114). Although Mao and Guevara represent considerably different political philosophies, their combined popularisation did much to encourage a similar play of categories in the minds of Western theorists. Guerrillas, it was argued, were representatives of the people. Terrorists were defined by an absence of this connection. This distinction between terrorist groups and guerrilla insurgencies continues to hold sway in modern conflicts; Ignacio Sanchez-Cuenca introduces his own quantitative study of political violence by describing how:

> Terrorism is political violence carried out by underground organizations that do not control part of the territory of the state in which they act. Guerrilla insurgencies, unlike terrorist organization, liberate territory, normally in the jungle or in the mountains, and rule this area. (2009, 689)

Such a distinction gives credence to the Guevarist principle of the *foco*. The *foco*, a military unit consisting of fewer than 12 guerrillas, attacks military targets in order to incite a military response. Once the process begins it merely falls to the *focos* to survive and let the military presence speak for itself. Aggressive counter-insurgency behaviour by the military inevitably upsets the locals, leading them to join the revolution. In the Cuban context this tactic resulted in Guevara's guerrillas gaining heroic underdog status in contrast to the Batista regime who became infamous for their cruelty. The theory has an undeniable appeal. Guevara's attempt to universalise the tactic and to replicate its effects in Bolivia and the Congo were not quite so successful, however, and the line between sabotage and terror—like Sorel's line between violence and force—was not always clear and distinct in practice.

The distinction between guerrilla and terrorist may indeed have remained a useful one were it to stand for rural and urban combatants respectively. Mao and Guevara undoubtedly privileged engagement with the peasantry over the traditional Marxist bloc of urban workers, trade unionists and intellectuals. Indeed, if we were to study only their actions it may not be at all relevant to include them in our potted history of terrorism. Yet what Mao and Guevara discouraged, the followers of Maoism and Guevarism would embrace wholeheartedly. From these ideologies the oxymoronic tactic of urban guerrilla warfare was brought into the world.

The urban guerrilla is a quintessentially 1970s phenomenon. It is born of the mistaken belief that the tactics of rural guerrilla warfare could be imported into the city, and it was popularised by its easy apologies for vanguardist violence. In the contemporary era there is no meaningful line that we could draw that would distinguish the urban guerrilla from the terrorist. Such is the flexibility of terror as a concept, however, that a line between them was firmly, if uncomfortably drawn during the 1970s. The urban guerrilla is the point where Marxist-Leninism and terrorism meet, and it's because of this historical nexus that this potted history takes the shape it does. As shall be seen, the ideological conflations which took place on the left in the 1970s encouraged sympathy for terrorism which is shocking when taken out of context. It is a good reason not to allow terrorism, an already malleable concept, to transgress the borders of meaning and become an empty signifier. The urban guerrilla construct is what happens when dangerous ideas become unmoored from the realities that brought them into existence.

The urban guerrilla was brought into being through the celebration of guerrilla warfare in general. The Guevarist *foco* was popularised in Regis Debray's *The Revolution in the Revolution?* (1967) and Mao's little red book of sayings flooded radical bookshops around the world. The theoretical transposition of guerrilla warfare into the urban setting was proposed by a number of writers, the most influential of which was Brazilian terrorist and bank robber Carlos Marighella. Marighella's *Mini-Manual of the Urban Guerrilla* (1969) extends Mao's "fish in water" metaphor to include streetwise youths and those on the borders of organised crime. He also conflated terrorism and other political violence within his theoretical introduction in a manner which would dismay dialecticians of the Marxist-Leninist tradition, arguing that:

> The accusation of 'violence' or 'terrorism' no longer has the negative meaning it used to have. It has acquired new clothing; a new colour. It does not divide, it does not discredit; on the contrary, it represents a centre of attraction. (2002, 3)

Marighella was killed in 1969, and his fellow leaders in the Brazilian urban guerrilla movement followed him in 1970 and 1971. Tactically, left-wing urban guerrilla terrorism intended to encourage a government crackdown: the subsequent authoritarian excesses would then act as a wake-up call to the people, who would rise up in response and bring about the revolution. In practice the Brazilian government did move to the right—Clutterbuck credits the terror with "[sabotaging] the prospect of a new and more liberal constitution" (1974, 255)—but the people did not rise up. Such results would become prophetic, as nowhere did the urban guerrilla tactic lead to revolution and, in those few places where it had minor success such as in Northern Ireland and the Basque country, it ultimately undermined the rule of law to such an extent that Terrorist Acts would be passed, habeas corpus suspended and a state of exception around terrorism would be normalised. Before this could occur in the West, however, the urban guerrilla had to be imported.

The emergence of urban guerrilla terrorism in the West can be partially explained by the collapse of 1960s prosperity and idealism into 1970s pessimism and stagnation, but it was also shaped by the conflicts in Vietnam and Algeria. Noam Chomsky has described these conflicts as teaching Western powers that "it was a mistake to employ a citizen's army to fight a brutal colonial war rather than mercenary forces, foreign or locally recruited, as had been traditional practice" (1988, 6). The soldiers fighting in Vietnam in particular weren't professionals there by choice but conscripted citizens, often with little sense of the specifics of the conflict. The revelation that Ho Chi Minh was leading an anti-imperialist uprising sowed the seeds of doubt to such an extent that radicals were drawn into uncritical acceptance of guerrilla tactics. Understanding begat apologism which, in its turn, begat support. Robert Taber's *The War of the Flea* (1970) celebrated armed insurrectionaries from across the globe with an emphasis on their triumphant Blanquist willpower:

> Limitations that were formerly accepted all at once become intolerable. The hint of imminent change suggests opportunities that had not been glimpsed until now. The will to act is born. It is as though people everywhere were saying: look, here is something we can do, or have, or be, simply by acting. Then what have we been waiting for? Let us act! (1970, 19)

The millenarianism of pre-Leninist terrorism returns as a salve to Western intellectuals. Mired in guilt for their country's actions overseas and finding no possibility of internal revolution the terrorist presents an alternative. In America this took the form of the Weathermen faction of the SDS (Students for a Democratic Society) who turned away from peaceful anti-war demonstrations to the fetishising of mass violence and disorder, causing riots like the Chicago "Days of Rage". These actions had no revolutionary function other than the destruction of property and the millenarian belief in the mass "wake-up" of the people. It is at this time that William Powell's *Anarchist Cookbook* (1971) became required illicit reading for American outcasts. Tariq Ali attributed this violence to young people "horrified by what [their] government was doing and who felt powerless" (1987, 216) but whose detachment from mainstream public feeling meant that their actions resulted every time in "total failure and isolation and repression" (1987, 217). As the decade progressed these groups grew smaller, and as failure piled upon failure the wafer-thin tactical justifications for urban guerrilla violence would give way to violence as a justification in and of itself. In each country the left-wing terror groups had their own historical contexts to draw upon, but each had in common their central tenet that violence represented commitment, and commitment had to be demonstrated through violence. The Weathermen brought about the Symbionese Liberation Front. The German anti-Vietnam movement gave birth to the Red Army Faction, or Baader-Meinhof Group. The Italian Autonomia movement had its Red Brigades and, facing them, the fascist New Order armed with weapons left behind after World War Two (Haberman). Even Britain had its Angry Brigade. The Japanese Red Army took this millenarianism to as yet unprecedented levels, conducting its own series of bloody internal purges to cleanse its ranks of those not sufficiently committed to the terrorist cause.

The political context of the 1970s was undoubtedly a complex one and to make judgments from the relative comfort of the contemporary era is always a critically dubious endeavour. I do not believe, however, that any but the most wilfully ahistorical analyses could consider the urban guerrilla theory to be anything but a colossal failure. Its practitioners verged between tragic heroes and farcical zealots. They held the pose of Camus' rebel, who rebels in order to rebel, and will find a cause wherever one lies:

> There is not one human being who, above a certain elementary level of consciousness, does not exhaust himself in trying to find formulae or attitudes which will give his existence the unity it lacks. Appearance and action, the dandy and the revolutionary, all demand unity, in order to exist and in order to exist on this earth. (1978, 228)

These strange poses could make stranger bedfellows, as Claire Sterling's best-selling *Terror Network* (1980) suggested. Although Sterling's paranoid work, which claimed all terrorism worldwide was being initiated and controlled from Moscow, was later revealed to be largely based on CIA propaganda, many of its stranger alliances contain kernels of truth. Tariq Ali travelled to Vietnam via Cuba courtesy of the Communist Party, the Red Army Faction trained with the Palestine Liberation

Organisation, Felix Guattari ran suitcases full of money across France for the Algerian underground, and infamous cannabis smuggler Howard Marks used the networks connecting British rock bands, the underground press and the IRA to create one of the biggest drug running operations of the era.

Sympathy for the potentially violent radical was sent up in its earliest years by Tom Wolfe in his account of a celebrity-packed, New York fundraiser for the Black Panthers which he christened "radical chic". "God, what a flood of taboo thoughts runs through one's head at these Radical Chic events," he wrote, "it is like the delicious shudder you get when you try to force the prongs of two horseshoe magnets together... *them* and *us*" (1971, 13). Indeed, the cover to November 1970s *Oz* magazine (No. 33) displays a similar satirical contempt for the fetishisation of armed revolution by elites. A hippy guerrilla, his submachine gun wielding lover and their beret-wearing baby snarl at the reader beside the tagline, "He drives a Maserati. She's a professional model. The boy is the son of the art editor of *Time* magazine. Some revolution!" That these models were young and well-off while posing as proletarian heroes is written off here as ludicrous posturing. Although, as we have seen from this short history of terrorism's roots, the terrorist phenomenon of the millenarian, Blanquist, voluntarist, spontaneist, existentialist, or whatever -ist type you wish to call it, is overwhelmingly associated with young people, predominantly but not exclusively male, and committed to violence as a means to keep the tricky world of real politics at bay. There is something ludicrous in the terrorist by default. Such a heightened level of commitment, especially to ideals which seem so self-evidently morally wrong, simply cannot sustain prolonged critical dissection. Yet it is this ludicrous single-mindedness which also makes the terrorist deadly, unwavering and unpredictable. It places them over a threshold where, sometime around the mid-1970s, governments of the West decided that they had transgressed the boundaries of criminality. The theory of the urban guerrilla, for all its foolishness, provokes the opposing excesses and illogics of Terrorism Acts. The category of terrorism becomes fixed in law but, in good Derridean style, it is this very fixity which allows its definition to slip away into linguistic ambiguity.

In the British case, the birth of terrorism legislation can be found in the unique situation presented by Northern Ireland. Martial law had long been a standard tactic in the colonies. Political violence was met by the suspension of habeas corpus and increased discretion to use violent means. The difference in Northern Ireland, however, was that a full reversion to martial law would effectively prove Sinn Fein's point for them. It would be an admission that Northern Ireland, like Ireland before it, was in its essence a colony rather than an extension of the United Kingdom. The British government had, if only for the purposes of propaganda, to maintain a semblance of the justice system under conditions which, in the colonies, would have undoubtedly have led to its suspension. The Northern Ireland (Emergency Provisions) Act of 1973 was the first of Britain's anti-terror legislations which, in retrospect, is very much the progenitor of the state of exception enshrined in Terrorism Acts after 2001. That the bill was signed into law prior to Operation Motorman is notable. The military objective of Motorman was to retake areas that Irish Republican Army (IRA) gunmen had made inaccessible to Royal Ulster Constabulary (RUC) policing, and from then on to support the police through a coordination of military force and police investigations. The new law created a similar overlapping of military and police jurisdiction by enforcing trial without jury for "scheduled offences" (Clutterbuck 1974, 147). Some of these offences were already crimes which would, in normal circumstances, be dealt with by the police: "murder, arson, assault, theft, robbery, making of possessing unauthorized lethal weapons and intimidation" (Clutterbuck 1974, 147). To these were added new offences such as "membership of any proscribed organization, publicly wearing [paramilitary] uniform, harbouring an escaper, and spying in aid of terrorism" (Clutterbuck 1974, 147). These offences bear a closer resemblance to the rules of the battlefield than those of law; they are drawing a line between enemy combatants and civilians. Yet this fusion of military and police did not result in a new legislative unity. The laws of war do not overlap with peacetime national laws: they are multinational, they transcend these laws; they legislate where national legislation ends. The offence of wearing paramilitary uniform, for example, is an attempt to identify a combatant. Combatants, however, exist in conflicts, not in peace. They are not, therefore, covered by peacetime laws, which the Emergency Provisions claimed to be. The uniform is a signifier of a conflict which the British government refused to define as a conflict. Uniform wearers are now subject to the punishment of the law in spite of having committed no crime by the standards of peacetime policing. The terrorist has, even in this early framing, become neither one thing nor the other. They are a criminal who has not yet committed a crime and a combatant who is not in a recognised conflict. The implication of these Emergency Provisions, no doubt written under duress, is that everyone involved knows to whom the laws are referring. The list of proscribed organisations is a starting point, but the Act extends to those who support them, who share their beliefs, or who simply act in ways that would aid them.

Grant Wardlaw, in his study of six country's experiences of terrorism, warns of the tendency for emergency provisions to be "too powerful. By overreacting or by failing to pull back after weakening the terrorists, the state itself may subvert democracy" (1994, 7). A particular danger, Wardlaw argues, is the targeting of extremism more broadly. If we take "democracy" to stand here for the free expression of political ideologies within some form of elective system then the anti-democratic potential that exists in the conflation of terrorism and political extremism is obvious. The fear of terrorism ends up silencing extreme opinions, making it very difficult to argue with them in the public sphere. Imran Awan argues that "many individuals once regarded as extremists are now considered high profile political activists and reformers" (2013, 6), and emphases how the incorporation of extremism into our definitions of what is or isn't terrorism has, in the British case at least, been a pivot point around which anti-terrorist discourse has managed to infringe upon otherwise peaceful political and religious beliefs. In particular he sees the post-2001 strand of Terrorism Acts as responsible for expanding the category of terrorist out of workable proportions. This begins with the use of the term "violent extremism". Although not synonymous with terrorism initially, long association made it appear so. The phrase "violent extremism" could then be loosened to merely refer to "extremism". "The PREVENT strand of [Britain's counterterrorism] strategy," is a key moment, he argues, when "the original phrase of 'violent extremism'" (2013, 6) loses its "violent" qualifier. This expansion aligns with dominant ideas regarding "hate speech"; a new category of law established in the same early-2000s moment that increased punishment for crimes with racist, religious or homophobic motives. Both sets of laws conflate crime and motivation. Whereas hate speech is illegal as it implies resentment against protected categories of people, extremism is illegal due to its implied resentment of the state. The removal of violence from the official definition of extremism suggests that violence has become synonymous with extremism (extremism *is* terrorism), or at least that the definition of violence has expanded to include so many non-violent acts that its presence is no longer valuable as a signifier. The use of certain words and phrases are now rhetorically considered to be violence, as, on occasion, are the omission of certain words and phrases. Silence itself can be violence, we are told. Under such conditions, accurately defining terrorism becomes a Sisyphean task.

Ultimately, as we enter the twenty-first century, terrorism as a category still exists in the ways that it did during the early twentieth century: terrorists still plant bombs and subscribe to theories of political violence. The definition has nevertheless crept, through extension and implication, into an area of fuzziness that presents a significant danger to democracy. For the linguist, especially the post-structuralist, there is room here to speculate endlessly upon the slippage of the signifier away from fixed meaning. However, one merely has to understand the basics of the terms' historical evolution to understand that its meaning is often clearly implied. Brian Blakemore's study of post-2012 Commons Select Committee reports on terrorism and the internet describes how a primary

> concern regarding cyber extremism is the process of self-radicalisation that occurs in isolation and how the messages and manipulation that can be found online may cause such predisposed individuals to initiate or progress their own self-radicalisation. (2013, 139)

The process being described here is that of reading or watching online videos and then having thoughts about them. These are basic human functions in a free society. Yet what the message is *really* saying is clear. "Self-radicalisation" refers to the adopting of extremist beliefs which, by extension, either lead to terrorism or are already a form of terrorism. What makes them extreme is their rejection of certain social values which the rest of us presumably share. According to Blakemore, any belief structure that rejects or opposes these values is extremism, and contemplating such beliefs is an act of self-radicalisation. But the police aren't targeting any theoretical belief structure; they are targeting the enemy, defined in quasi-military terms. Muslim combatants, predominantly, are an enemy, but so still are the Northern Irish paramilitaries; the communist threat has been replaced by Antifa and the eco-warriors, the far-right are still around, as angry and incomprehensible as ever, and, as for all other forms of extremism—vegans, scientologists, Millwall fans, Cornish separatists—one can safely presume that, in spite of being within the extremist category of the law, M15 will spend no time or resources pursuing and monitoring them.

In fact, the question of monitoring appears itself to be somewhat of a red herring. The laxness of terrorism's definition may have opened the legislative door to spy programmes like PRISM (US) and Tempora (UK) but our intelligence service's real work is in the construction of data processing machines. Their programs, capable of sifting and channelling avalanches of metadata, bear little resemblance to the phone-tapping and undercover operatives of the 1970s. Terrorists really do exist, but it often appears that our contemporary anti-terrorism agencies have long outgrown them. Like the term itself, they have expanded into areas nearby. In the age of WikiLeaks one almost suspects that the initial shock caused by Snowden's revelations will give way to cynicism and normalization and terrorism, having fulfilled its usefulness as a term, will shrink back down to its original proportions. It will refer again to political violence either by the state (*à la* Robespierre), against the state (*à la* Sorel), or as a more niche category of the above. This, however, is purely speculation. What is of importance for this particular study are the ways in which terrorism came to be conceptualized in the literature of the 1970s. With this in mind we will turn briefly to two key factors underlying the terrorist narratives that are being studied. Firstly, the question of belief and commitment; terrorism describing a process of rational political beliefs leading to irrational actions. Secondly, terrorism as an enactment of narrative itself; something which comes about under certain circumstances and fatalistically plays out in near-symmetrical ways across texts. Bearing this in mind, we can finally start to address the novels themselves, taking nothing for granted and not relying on cliché.

NARRATIVES OF TERROR: LOOKING BACK FROM NOW

In the years following the World Trade Centre attacks of 2001 and the subsequent invasions of Afghanistan and Iraq, dismissal of terrorism as a specialist category was a common line of argument taken by liberal critics of the Bush Doctrine. "We need to 'de-fang' terrorism," as Mary Patten phrased it, "to coolly understand it as a tactic of warfare that has been used for thousands of years" (2010, 12–13). Terrorism kills fewer people than toilets, and certainly far fewer people are killed by terrorists than by, say, police officers (Harper 2012). The implications of this argument were that government responses to the threat of terrorism were therefore not proportional in that they restricted liberties and expanded the surveillance state. The importance of these arguments within the scheme of our own study is the extent to which they reflect the state of the post-globalised world. If terrorism arose with the modern state, as we've seen, then terrorism as an existential threat in itself is tied to the unipolar condition of the world following the collapse of communism. The project of globalisation was premised upon the final victory of capitalism, and aimed at the creation of a world market. Ideologically, free-market cheerleaders conceived of a world market as a recipe for world peace, although the causation is likely the other way around: American military hegemony ended large-scale conflicts, bringing about conditions conducive to free markets. By conceiving the markets as drivers of peace and prosperity, globalised politics took a distinctly technocratic turn in its discourse. Terrorism, following the liberal argument, was not a significant enough threat to warrant management by state actors. Such an argument was a reactive one, however, which did little to dispel the dominant conception of terrorism as an existential threat. It is this view which influenced the policies of both the Bush and the Obama eras. Under the technocratic terms of these governments' actual policies (setting aside for a moment the "Clash of Civilisations" narrative used to promote them), terrorism was conceived as the natural enemy of the stable world order. The War on Terror therefore resembled the policing actions of previous wars on drugs and gangs rather than wars between states or ideologies. America, it was presumed, stood not for an ideology, but for modernity and the universal values of freedom. These universal values stood against the anti-Enlightenment beliefs of terrorists.

Terrorism as it is conceived in the post-globalisation era can therefore come to take the position of belief in general. World markets are presented as rational, not based on beliefs but facts, and are threatened by the believing other. The particular political configurations of Islamic fundamentalism—the very different cases of Wahhabism, Islamic State or the Muslim Brotherhood, to give examples—tend to be of little interest in counter-terror literature. David C. Rapoport, in writing of terror as a form of "messianic belief" (1988, 196) describes how:

> The messianic believer thinks that he must participate in a struggle to 'force the end,' the nature of the messianic aspiration itself or the cause will become a factor conducive to terror… it would seem rather obvious

that, when the stakes of any struggle are perceived as being great, the conventional restraints on violence diminish accordingly. (1988, 204)

Beliefs, provided they are deeply held and are acted upon, are positioned as antithetical to peace and stability. The more one believes the less one restrains one's violent tendencies. Herein lies the root of "extremism" as a concept; a single idea that unites personal belief and violent action. Walter Lacqueur shares this conception of what he calls "new terrorism... indiscriminate in the choice of its victims" (9), unlike the old terrorism "discriminate, selecting its victims carefully—kings and queens, government ministers, generals" (2003, 9). There is some truth in this, although where Lacqueur and Rapoport along with many others frame this as a phenomenon brought about by the terrorists alone, a reflexive consideration of how this argument is also framed by globalized policing will allow us to comprehend this as a mode of terrorism peculiar to our time. The unipolar world implicates opposition in a universal struggle. This could not be the case under the bipolar conditions of the Cold War. Al Qaida's tactics learn from the guerrilla experience—using terror as a way of forcing the state to reveal its "hidden totalitarianism"—but they don't present a political alternative, only the fall of America as an end in itself. The failure of Islamic State's attempt to build "Islamism in one country" emphasises how Islamic fundamentalism is framed by its opposition to modernity; it doesn't offer an alternative future, only a pure negation of what it conceives as a Westernised future.

In terms of narrative, the twenty-first century positions terrorism as just another narrative of belief equating to madness, whether Quixotic or monstrous. The postmodern fear of "metanarratives" is one mode by which the humanities could comprehend terrorism. Another, more dangerous one, involved the grouping of Islamist terrorists alongside other "micronarratives" opposing the "metanarrative" of capitalism. Daniel T. O'Hara argues for seeing post-9/11 narratives in this way; "the abstract homogeneity of the global market economy and its rapid and devastating flows of capital," he argues, "define the general parameters for an oppositional array of pre-established group identities" (2007, 56). There is something here of Thomas Pynchon's conspiratorial fantasy; the Black Panthers and the KKK working together against racial integration, Islamic militants and libertarian communists fighting together against the shared enemy of liberal complacency. And, as with postmodern literature, terrorism is soon reduced to signs and signifiers; "wars have become 'postmodern' and 'discursive'," as Houen argues, "its unity is rhetorical. What categorizes it are the metaphors and symbols that structure it" (2001, 4). Under these conditions, "producing a narrative or theory that outlines an aetiology of terrorism and accounts for its effects is obviously a form of counterterrorism in itself" (2001, 11). I have argued in a previous paper (Darlington 2016) that the most critically acclaimed novels dealing with terrorism published in the first decade following 9/11—DeLillo's *Falling Man* (2005), Jonathan Foer's *Extremely Loud and Incredibly Close* (2005)—were written by established postmodern authors whose literary productions demonstrated no conceptual break from earlier works. Postmodernist concepts prevalent in the globalising 1990s transferred easily into the post-9/11 world. This, in spite of the commonly held belief that 9/11 "changed everything". History, in these novels, has still ended, it's just that certain Muslims haven't had the sense to recognise it yet. Now, it may be that the Arab Spring and the complexities of the Syrian civil war have done much to complicate our conceptions of the world, and the rise of populism in the West has challenged the presumptions of neo-liberalism directly, yet our contemporary understanding of terrorism is undoubtedly framed by what remains of the postmodern.

In order to return our historical imagination to the 1970s and grasp the meaning of terrorism as it appeared *then*, there are some key moments which we can use to help situate our understanding. Firstly, the Cold War was still the predominant mode by which global politics was understood. Terrorists in a bipolar world still fight the powers that be but, by implication, they are also perceived to be in support of the system conceived as opposite, even if this was not entirely the case. The IRA embraced a form of socialism during the 1970s that, although not pro-USSR, was certainly anti-British. The conflicts of the Third World, caught between socialism and capitalism, were framed in these terms, making strange bedfellows as America funded religious extremists and the Soviets propped up African dictators. Claire Sterling's *The Terror Network* (1980) took the decade's bipolaric paranoia to its logical extreme and tied every terrorist group in the world back to the machinations of Kremlin agents. This paranoid framework was, for British audiences, bolstered on one side by the perceived collapse of the British Empire and on the other by the 1973 economic downturn. The recession was sparked by an Oil Crisis manufactured by the Gulf States and was prolonged by militant conflicts between labour and capital. The hope and prosperity of the mid-60s became the political turbulence of 1968 which, after the crash and its attendant disillusionment, became intransigence and bitterness. The period we now look back on as "the post-war consensus" had definitively ended. It is under these conditions that British writers of the 1970s turned to the figure of the terrorist as a potent symbol; and not a symbol of total otherness, or of impossible beliefs, but very often as a sympathetic figure, a person like us who has allowed themselves to act. Most importantly, when compromise appears to have become impossible and the political system as it exists seems like a totally immovable object— when there is no hope, in other words—then the terrorist comes to stand in for questions of conviction and agency. The terrorist is often presented as stuck between acting on their beliefs, even if such action is futile, or else renouncing those beliefs when confronted by a complex world. The terrorist becomes a Hamlet, asking whether 'tis nobler in the mind to suffer the slings and arrows of outrageous fortune or to take arms against a sea of troubles. By opposing their troubles, however, the terrorist rarely ends them: they oppose simply to oppose.

In bringing to a close this initial overview I move now from establishing the historical and conceptual groundwork to proposing my own schema. In reading the 60 or so novels which make up the subject of this work a particular narrative structure recurred on a very regular basis. This structure will be referred to throughout this work as the "standard terrorist morphology", and, in its morphological form, it can be described like so:

(1) *Ideological Education*. The protagonist is introduced to the struggle. The issues at the heart of the narrative are explained. Very often this education is by a member of the opposite sex although it can also come from a figure representing political experience. The cause is presented sympathetically through exposition aimed at educating the unfamiliar reader.

(2) *Activism*. In pursuing and promoting their new ideological cause the protagonist undertakes actions that increase in dramatic intensity as the narrative progresses. Typical first actions include leafleting or graffiti, which build to marches, occupations and other acts which draw the ire of the police and/or other state forces.

(3) *Loss of Innocence*. A violent encounter with the police and/or other state forces convinces the protagonist of their enmity to the powers that be and that the rightness of their cause can justify the

use of violence. The actions of the powers that be are presented as unfair, excessive and often illegal in order to encourage the reader to sympathise with the protagonist's inner turmoil.
(4) *Radicalisation*. Convinced of the need to use violence to achieve their cause, the protagonist finds themselves on one side of a split within their group, alienating former allies, friends and/or family. A major operation is planned which has the potential to bring about a resolution to their struggle. Their horizon narrows such that they (and by extension the novel's narrative) focus on this plan to the exclusion of all others.
(5) *The Last Moment*. At the very last moment a change of heart is experienced by the protagonist, or else a happy accident occurs, or an oversight from earlier comes back to bite them, or the detective antagonist arrives just in time: whatever the cause, the plan fails at the last second and the protagonist is, to an extent, redeemed as a tragic figure rather than a pure villain.

The standard terrorist morphology recurs so often that it would not be worth listing the novels in this study which conform to it. Overall, they are in the majority, although some conform to it more strictly than others. Whether this typical narrative might apply in other contexts is not the concern of this current study, although I personally do not believe that it has any bearing on twenty-first century terrorist novels, at least not to such an extent as to be "standard". The particular historical conditions of Britain in the 1970s, the bipolar global politics that frame it, and the longer history of terrorism as concept and tactic which preceded it (not to mention the conventions of the thriller genre) are all visible in these stories. They offer an alternative perspective on terror, but one as situated in its moment as our own society's predominant views are situated in our own moment. Further research may discover other texts which conform to the structure but for now it falls to us to address the novels themselves.

Bibliography

Ali, Tariq. 1987. *Street Fighting Years: An Autobiography of the Sixties*. London: Collins.
Awan, Imran. 2013. Extremism, Radicalisation and Terrorism. In *Extremism, Counter-Terrorism and Policing*, ed. Imran Awan and Brian Blakemore. London: Ashgate.

Barker, Jonathan. 2003. *The No-Nonsense Guide to Terrorism*. London: New Internationalist.
Blakemore, Brian. 2013. Trends and the Postmodernist Extremist. In *Extremism, Counter-Terrorism and Policing*, ed. Imran Awan and Brian Blakemore. London: Ashgate.
Burke, Edmund. 1986. *Reflections on the Revolution in France*. London: Penguin.
———. 2008. *A Philosophical Enquiry into the Origin of Our Ideas of the Sublime and the Beautiful*. Oxford: Oxford University Press.
Camus, Albert. 1978. *The Rebel*, trans. Anthony Bower. London: Penguin.
Chomsky, Noam. 1988. *The Culture of Terrorism*. London: Pluto Press.
Clutterbuck, Richard. 1974. *Protest and the Urban Guerrilla*. New York: Abelard-Schuman.
Danzell, Orlandrew E. 2011. Political Parties: When Do They Turn to Terror? *Journal of Conflict Resolution* 55 (1): 85–105.
Darlington, Joseph. 2016. Capitalist Mysticism and the Historicising of 9/11 in Thomas Pynchon's Bleeding Edge. *Critique: Studies in Contemporary Fiction* 47 (3): 242–253.
Guevara, Ernesto. 2009. *Guerrilla Warfare: The Authorised Edition*. London: Harper Perennial.
Haberman, Clyde. 1990. Evolution in Europe; Italy Discloses Its Web of Cold War Guerrillas. *The New York Times*. Web: http://www.nytimes.com/1990/11/16/world/evolution-in-europe-italy-discloses-its-web-of-cold-war-guerrillas.html. Accessed 16 Nov 1990.
Harper, Jim. 2012. You're Eight Times More Likely to Be Killed by a Police Officer Than a Terrorist. *Cato at Liberty*. Cato Institute. Web: https://www.cato.org/blog/youre-eight-times-more-likely-be-killed-police-officer-terrorist. Accessed 10 Aug 2012.
Houen, Alex. 2001. *Terrorism and Modern Literature*. Oxford: Oxford University Press.
Laqueur, Walter. 1975. The Origins of Guerrilla Doctrine. *Journal of Contemporary History* 10 (3): 341–382.
———. 2003. *No End to War: Terrorism in the Twenty-First Century*. London: Continuum.
Lenin, V.I. 1986. The State and Revolution: Experience of the Paris Commune of 1871. Marx's Analysis. In *The Essential Works of Lenin*, ed. Henry M. Christman. New York: Dover.
Lih, Lars T. 2011. *Lenin*. London: Reaktion Books.
Marighella, Carlos. 2002. *Mini-Manual of the Urban Guerrilla*. Montreal: Arm the Spirit Press.
O'Hara, Daniel T. 2007. 'The Cry of Its Occasion': On the Subject of Truth; or, The Terror in Global Terrorism. *Boundary 2* 34 (2): 55–69.

Patten, Mary. 2010. What Is to Be (Un)Done: Notes on Teaching Art and Terrorism. *Radical Teacher* 89: 9–20.

Rapoport, David C. 1988. Messianic Sanctions on Terror. *Comparative Politics* 20 (2): 195–213.

Robespierre, Maximilien. 2007a. On the Principles of Political Morality That Should Guide the National Convention in the Domestic Administration of the Republic [1974]. In *Virtue and Terror*, ed. Jean Ducange, trans. John Howe. London: Verso.

———. 2007b. Response of the National Convention to the Manifestos of the Kings Allied Against the Republic [1793]. In *Virtue and Terror*, ed. Jean Ducange, trans. John Howe. London: Verso.

Sanchez-Cuenca, Ignacio. 2009. Revolutionary Dreams and Terrorist Violence in the Developed World: Explaining Country Variation. *Journal of Peace Research* 46 (5): 687–706.

Sorel, Georges. 2004. *Reflections on Violence* [1906], trans. T.E. Hulme and J. Roth. New York: Dover.

Taber, Robert. 1970. *The War of the Flea: Guerrilla Warfare Theory and Practice*. St Albans: Paladin.

Tse-Tung, Mao. 2007. *On Guerrilla Warfare*, trans. Samuel B. Griffith. New York: BN Publishing.

Wardlaw, Grant. 1994. The Democratic Framework. In *The Deadly Sin of Terrorism: Its Effect on Democracy and Civil Liberty in Six Countries*, ed. David A. Charters. London: Greenwood Press.

Wolfe, Tom. 1971. *Radical Chic and Mau-Mauing the Flak Catchers*. New York: Bantam.

CHAPTER 3

The Terrorist Novel, Thrillers and Postcolonial Britain

A study of the phenomenon here labelled the "terrorist novel" has to begin with the thriller. The great majority of British novels featuring terrorists published in the 1970s take this form, with exceptions to the rule often making knowing nods toward established genres to highlight their conscious divergence. If the terrorist figure were to be isolated as a distinct element of iconography, the thriller would be the form it represented. Unlike "sci-fi" or "western", however, the thriller sits uneasily as a distinct genre. As Martin Rubin describes it, "the range of stories that have been called thrillers is simply too broad" (1999, 4). The same can be said of those thrillers specifically featuring terrorists as protagonists, characters, or plot devices. To carve meaning from this diverse array of texts, this chapter will concentrate on a small collection indicative of wider trends within the form or else exemplary works stylistically. Two such exemplary texts are Graham Greene's *The Honorary Consul* (1973) and V.S. Naipaul's *Guerrillas* (1975). Both works transcend the common pitfalls of the thriller; either over-complication making for convoluted storytelling, or over-simplification which reinforces brute stereotypes (*The Levanter* stands as our example of the first, *The Chilian Club* the second). Greene and Naipaul also represent the 1970s terrorist novel's deepest engagements with the legacy of Empire. This legacy casts a shadow over the entire form, regardless of specific settings or narratives. For the sake of structure, this chapter will address thrillers set outside Britain in the first half, and those addressing the British nation in the

© The Author(s) 2018
J. Darlington, *British Terrorist Novels of the 1970s*,
https://doi.org/10.1007/978-3-319-77896-9_3

second half. However, it is undeniable that each facet—the national and international—influences the other on a symbolic level.

TERROR, THRILLER, FACT AND FICTION

Situating thrillers as a form in the 1970s, Katy Fletcher makes a clear case for an increasing complexity and ambiguity of subject matter occurring across the Anglophone world. In America, Cold War narratives moved away from fantasies of Russian invasion or nuclear holocaust and focused more upon proxy wars or intrigues in "isolated areas of the world" (1987, 319). In Britain a similar shift was represented in a variety of satirical attacks on the James Bond franchise and its imitators, while John le Carre and Fredrick Forsyth injected "a cold dose of cynicism" (1987, 319) into the bestseller lists. Fletcher argues that much of this complexity can be attributed to the mid-1970s congressional investigations into the CIA which made the public "better informed about espionage practices. Readers of spy fiction are now familiar with spy jargon and tradecraft techniques" (1987, 322). One must also, however, place these revelations in the context of guerrilla warfare's ascendancy. *The Anarchist Cookbook* (1971) is a clear example of an American writer looking to turn espionage "tradecraft techniques" to terrorist purpose. The potential power of guerrilla insurgency, already learned by the British in Cyprus and Palestine, was made very clear to Americans in their final defeat by the Vietnamese in 1975. The real world of the 1970s was becoming ever harder to explain in simple ideological terms and the shift towards complexity, intrigue and cynicism is an expression of the uncertainties plaguing the developed world's sense of itself.

The line between fiction and purported fact must also be considered when studying the terrorist thriller and some of the connections being made by investigative journalism in the 1970s. At the peak of 1970s paranoia, pseudo-events and dodgy presumptions regularly made headlines and filled editorial columns. The peak of conflation between outright propaganda and historical fact can be found in Claire Sterling's *The Terror Network*, appearing in 1980 as a narrative tying together the endless complex strands of terrorist and guerrilla activity during the previous decade and making them into a Cold War thriller. From a complex whole, Sterling argues each element can be tied back (often very tangentially) to those pulling the strings in Moscow. Described as having "a history of running CIA black propaganda" (2009, 229) by Nick

Davies, Sterling's blurring of the line between fact and fiction was seemingly confirmed by Melvin Goodman, Head of the Office of Soviet Affairs in the CIA himself in Adam Curtis' 2004 documentary *The Power of Nightmares*, wherein the book is dismissed as at least half invention. Of special interest are the literary influences that can be traced behind some of these spurious connections. Stories which begin in fiction reappear as fact. Sterling's invention surrounding Henri Curiel is a notable example. Curiel's activities involved financially and diplomatically supporting third world liberation movements such as the Algerian FLN and South African ANC and are well documented in Gilles Perrault's (1987) biography. These, arguably, were not uncommon for a member of the French far-left at this time. In Sterling's version, Curiel operates "something politically chic and vaguely charitable called *Aide de Amite* (Help and Friendship)" (1981, 50) which acts a safehouse-come-communications centre for international terrorism. The description of this five-star guerrilla stopover in a sophisticated Paris merchant district bears an incredible resemblance to FIRCO, the "charitable organisation" (1981, 56), *Fraternite Internationale de la Resistance Contre l'Oppression* which appears in the James Bond novel *Thunderball* (1961) as the headquarters of his arch-nemeses SPECTRE: "The Special Executive for Counterintelligence, Terrorism, Revenge and Extortion" (2012, 69).[1] Whether Sterling's rendering of *Aide de Amite* can be tied back directly to Fleming's *l'Fraternite Internationale* is impossible to say, although a more troubling connection can be found between the *Agius Demetrios*—a Palestinian ship loaded with TNT and forty-two Katyusha rockets sank by the Israeli navy in 1978—and the plot of Eric Ambler's *The Levanter* (1972). In Sterling's report on the *Agius* incident the Palestinians planned to fire the rockets at Eilat's oil refinery, "set the ship's automatic pilot to head straight for the crowded beach, and make their getaway to Jordan" (1973, 280). Other than the substitution of the Eilat oil refinery for the Tel Aviv coast, the story is identical to the one Ambler published six years earlier, right down to the choice of a Greek ship as cover.[2] The *Agius Demetrios* incident is notable as, if the details are true, it could mean either that Ambler's thriller successfully predicted a terrorist incident or, even more worryingly, that Ambler's seemingly far-fetched narrative directly inspired an audacious action by real-life guerrillas. It is an indicator of the kinds of confusion abounding in the 1970s around terrorisms, real and imagined, that historical fact seems to shift and sway in the breeze of ideology. The thriller doesn't exist in a vacuum but in a semiological dance with the intelligence community, imparting it with a structure of feeling on the one hand while drawing practical information out of it on the other. On rare occasions, the thriller has even been known to return the favour; providing intelligence services with new insights through its speculative realism.

Fletcher has commented on how the thriller, most especially in its espionage forms, can play a dangerous role in shaping reader's responses to reality:

> The spy novel is essentially written for entertainment and read as a form of escapism. The spy novel is not compelled to be realistic, or even plausible, except that unlike science fiction, it claims to represent the real political world. The possible danger in this kind of literature lies in the attitudes the spy novel projects in building up a generally false image of the real world. (1987, 321)

The political implications of this role extend beyond the possibility of fiction interfering with historical facts or the specifics of intelligence and counterintelligence. The influential power of the thriller derives from its elevation of particular characters and stock-types into archetypes standing in for Britain's relationship with the rest of the world. The escapism of a triumphant Empire embodies itself in heroic colonisers unambiguously asserting their superiority. The hero of postcolonial Britishness, however, is closer to a rather maudlin trickster figure; inhabiting the dark spaces of contradiction and insecurity with low cunning and ever-increasing cynicism. No matter its relationship to empirical reality or commitment to realism, the figure of the terrorist in 1970s British literature invokes the threatened nation and mobilises a scattered array of images from the national imaginary in response.

Graham Greene, Empire and Belief

For Graham Greene in *The Honorary Consul* (1973), the decaying remains of the British Empire appear as signifiers vacant of what former meaning they had. They are not the only institution that has fallen from grace, however. The book is riven with tensions between language and belief, and between belief and action, specifically the English language and Catholic belief. The head of the guerrilla cell in the novel, Leon Rivas, who stands in as the terrorist's voice of reason, embodies these inner conflicts. Rivas was first trained as a lawyer, then a priest, before finally turning revolutionary:

> Doctor Plarr remembered how first there had been the law books Leon studied – he had once explained to him the meaning of tort. Then there had been all the works of theology – Leon was able to make even the Trinity seem plausible by a sort of higher mathematics. He supposed there must be other primers to read in the new life. Perhaps he was quoting Marx. (2004, 98)

The legalistic approach to the literal letter of first the law, then the Church, and then the revolution all appears as a sort of empty gesturing, and it is the sense of all gestures ultimately returning to us empty which underpins Greene's novel. Through language Rivas is attempting to mould the world into his own image while, to the cynical and world-weary protagonist Doctor Plarr, all institutions and ideologies appear hopeless and their operations ultimately futile. Anthony Burgess identifies Greene's Catholicism at the route of these doubts, and ascribes this doubt an "international character". It is the Catholic struggle with faith which ultimately establishes "the politics of Greene [as] world politics" (1967, 95). Faith in the Eucharist as miracle not metaphor, and the spiritual struggle this entails, also reflects the fate of post-war nationhood and, by extension, imperialism. The Empire is a ritual; a power structure which exists in the reality of its language and signs. Once the British stop believing in it, the structures of thought and interpretation still linger everywhere, haunting British culture's vision of the world just as the religious framework imparted by the Church continues to structure the apostate's imagination even when faith is lost. The novel's negotiation of faith and Englishness on an existential level elevate its terrorist thriller narrative to a rumination on the nature of postcolonial belief.

Greene's particular post-lapsarian despair can be traced through his real-life encounters with revolutionary figures. During the 1960s, when Greene's faith in Catholicism was already subject to doubt, he appears to project his hopes onto heroes of the counterculture: Ho Chi Minh and Fidel Castro being most notable. Meeting Ho Chi Minh, he describes his "kind, remorseless face [which] had no fanaticism about it. A man is a fanatic about a mystery—tablets of stone, a voice from a burning bush— but this was a man who had patiently solved an equation" (1969a, 402). The communist takes on the appearance of a religious figure, but specifically a figure in the Catholic model: one who understands the need for structure, hierarchy and order. Castro too, "so Pauline in his labours, [is said to have] a quality of generosity which calls for loyalty" (1969b, 412). During this period, Greene appears to hold out hope that a non-Soviet Marxism might offer an alternative to a fallen capitalism and a corrupted communism. "Cuba may well become the real testing ground of Communism" (1969b, 411), he argues. By the 1970s, however, the "test" he is hopeful for is judged to have failed. In conversation with Marie Francois-Allain Greene admits that "Communism is unlikely ever to escape from Stalinism or dictatorship" (1981, 95); his faith in what Brennan has called the "combined conservatism and subversion" (2016, xi) of both Marxism and Catholicism has now been lost. The Empire might be a hollow signifier, but so are Marx and the Bible now. These grand internationalist ideas are presented as the Quixotic dreams of flawed individuals.

Greene's post-internationalist disillusionment is shared by the protagonist of the novel, Doctor Eduardo Plarr. The half-Paraguayan son of an English father, Plarr is forever overshadowed by this Anglo-Saxon anti-imperialist who died for his political beliefs. This seeming self-sacrifice is an act Plarr can never bring himself to fully understand, preferring instead to play the pastiched role of a reserved and aloof Englishman, worldly-wise and cynical in his judgements. Early in the novel he tips off his old school friend Rivas as to the whereabouts of an American consul Rivas' terrorist group seeks to kidnap. Following a mix-up, Rivas and his gang instead capture Charley Fortnum, one of only three Englishmen in the region, who just happens to hold the ornamental title of "Honorary Consul": a powerless office awarded for a vague service to the monarchy many years ago. Fortnum is regarded as a total embarrassment by the British authorities due to his chronic alcoholism, general incompetence and recent wedding to a very young girl he met while she was working at a brothel. Doctor Plarr, compelled by guilt after his role in the kidnap (as well as a half-hearted affair he pursued with Fortnum's young bride) decides to set about rescuing the honorary consul only to find himself stuck between the intransigence and confusion of both sides; terrorist and state. As Barbara Lakin summarises the calamity, "absurdity is not too strong a word to describe the terrorists' wasted efforts. On the other hand, the British government, far from sending out the troops to save the consuls who become victims of the terrorists, would be glad to be rid of their services" (1986, 70). Fortnum, whose position as honorary consul signifies absolutely nothing is helped by no-one in the community but Plarr—a man whose world-weary actions betray a constitutional inability to believe in any cause—and the means of that rescue are embodied in an attempt to demonstrate to the guerrillas the absurdity of their own beliefs. As a last act of ritual, the now-atheist Rivas conducts a mass on their final morning before they are all gunned down by military forces. Only the inept Fortnum survives, living on to continue his role as a functionless symbol of Empire.

Alongside Fortnum's meaningless title, over which the final massacre ultimately results, the novel is stocked with an array of signifiers for Englishness which each betray a fundamental lack of depth. Rather than his breviary, Rivas confides to Plarr that the only book he carries with him is an English detective story. For him, the detective novel represents a secular faith as superstitious as a religious one, "the story of a dream-world where justice is always done" (2004, 204). He describes the London of the novel as "a wonderful peaceful world… everything is so well ordered. There are no problems. There is an answer to every question" (2004, 205). Yet, upon asking the deeper meaning of the main character's surname "Bradshaw", he discovers it only to be a family name, an empty tradition, and asks, "King's Cross. Would that be symbolic?" "No. Just the name of a station" (2004, 209). Like religious practices, the symbols of Britishness which are ascribed hidden meaning by the foreigner Rivas are revealed to be arbitrary and depthless.

Finding that seemingly sacred names have no power is a lesson also learned by Plarr and Fortnum's fellow townspeople as they attempt to establish an "English Club"; suggesting that a telegram from the English Club to *The Times* or *Telegraph* would provoke "some Opposition M.P. who will take [their cause] up" (2004, 133). With only a handful of members, however, the Club still manages to argue over the wording of the telegram and decide that Fortnum's cause is "such small beer" (2004, 133) that they would struggle to have it published at all. Both Rivas' expectations regarding English nomenclature and the failure of the English Club plan reveal the supposedly deep and meaningful call of British civilisation to ultimately lack a signified presence. Like Fortnum's consistent tendency to fly the Union Jack upside down, the legacy of the British Empire in Greene's South America is one in which all semblance of power is lost and even the hollow symbols which remain are confusing and disheartening to the ones who wield them.

Against this all-pervasive apathy, Greene poses only two clear models for hope and redemption. One is the atheistical Rivas who at least performs the rituals of the Church, if not with the requisite faith. The other is the Argentine writer, Doctor Saavedra, whose hackneyed tales of overwrought *machismo* are popular among readers but mocked and satirised by younger writers and critics. Initially incredulous as to Saavedra's romantic posturing, Plarr is shocked when he visits the writer's house in the poverty-stricken *barrio*:

> He felt a new respect for Doctor Saavedra. His obsession with literature was not absurd whatever the quality of his books. He was willing to suffer poverty for its sake, and a disguised poverty was far worse to endure than an open one. The effort needed to polish his shoes, to press his suit… He couldn't, like the young, let things go. Even his hair must be cut regularly. A missing button would reveal too much. (2004, 158)

Saavedra represents the only legitimate authenticity within the novel. His commitment to literature is total, as embodied in his meticulous sartorial upkeep where not a single hair is out of place. His struggle is that of the Company's Chief Accountant in Conrad's *Heart of Darkness* whose pristine "starched collars and got-up shirt-fronts were achievements of character… in the great demoralisation of the land he kept up his appearance" (1994, 26). A singleness of purpose which is tied directly to outward signs of respectability, albeit in a metaphorical manner, makes for an absolute confidence of identity. Catholic identity, revolutionary identity, and especially British identity, suffer constant disappointments and disillusions as the novel progresses, becoming deeply unstable if not falling apart altogether. Saavedra's faith in literature is presented as the only unwavering identity and yet, like Quixote, his absolute confidence is a comic one. Saavedra is certain in his identity as only a foreign entity can be. The human quality of Greene's characters can be found in their flaws, with the terrorist actions of insurgents reduced to one of a series of great mistakes, misunderstandings and bungles. In this way, Greene's terrorists share in the tragedy of belief in an age of pessimism. The more glorious something appears when you believe in it, the narrative argues, the more ridiculous it appears when you don't.

V.S. Naipaul and Empire's Long Shadow

The disillusion present in Greene's *The Honorary Consul* is a misleadingly teleological one, however. It has a finality to it familiar to post-war British writers as the infamous end of Empire. In Greene's world the guerrilla takes part in a struggle which has already been lost, as all struggles must inevitably be lost in this era of endings. In the other great terrorist novel of the British 1970s, V.S. Naipaul's *Guerrillas* (1976), there is at once a deeper pessimism but also a more ambiguous picture of the continuing pervasion of Western power under postcolonial circumstances. Naipaul's guerrillas play a minor part in the political arena much like Greene's, but that part plays out amidst the turbulence of third world power politics still indebted to global geopolitical networks of influence. Anne R. Zahlan argues that Naipaul's novels of the 1970s "constitute embittered assaults on the social and political chaos that has succeeded empire" (1994, 89) due to their overwhelming concern with entropy and decay in post-liberation settings. In *Guerrillas*, however, one can arguably locate behind the cynical posturing of defeated activists a dissection of how the discursive subjectification of Third World struggles shapes them into idealised Eurocentric forms. The terrorist struggling against Western imperialism strives to embody the heroic image created by Western anti-imperialism. The relationship between developed and developing world is embodied in the two figures of Roche, the one-time anti-apartheid terrorist turned cynical, and Jimmy Ahmed, the Maoist guerrilla preaching back-to-the-land communism. With terrorists as both protagonist and antagonist, Naipaul's text can interrogate cultural constructions of revolutionary violence with a clearer sense of historical-political specificity than Greene's universalising prerogative allows for.

In addressing Naipaul's novel and its guerrilla antagonist, critics have often argued for a universalising approach. Zahlen describes how "revolution gives way to dispirited personal violence: one murder on one island takes the place of the 'universal bloodshed' associated with apocalypse" (1994, 103). Neil ten Kotenaar traces the allegorical qualities of the novel back to its source material, the self-styled black revolutionary Abdul Malik whose murder conviction in 1972 is echoed in Jimmy Ahmed's rape and murder of the white liberal Jane at the novel's bloody climax. According to Kotenaar:

Malik used the words that he picked up in liberal London to give himself a character; they were mere tokens he could fill with whatever meaning he chose to give them. An ability to manipulate words and others' impressions of him allowed him to create a heroic role for himself. However, the hollowness of his words also allowed him to hide even from himself and prevented him from ever expressing himself fully. (1990, 324–325)

It is this postcolonial mimicry of militant discourse which carries the tragic resonance necessary for "one murder on one island" to come to represent a whole field of conflicted ideological transmission. The struggle for political and economic self-determination in the third world during the 1970s was comprehended by first and second world alike as a factor of a larger Cold War dichotomy. To find that these discourses have been adopted in their turn as a cover for brutal, non-politically oriented violence presents the first world reader with an uncanny mirror image of their own ideological inauthenticities. As Meredith, a former slave-owner, says of Jimmy Ahmed: "He's dangerous because he's famous, because he has a lot of that English glamour still, and because he's nothing at all… anybody can use that man and make chaos in this place. He can be programmed" (1976, 140). Yet when Jimmy writes in his diary of his exploits with a childish voice—half-revolutionary, half-Victorian novel—one does not get the feeling of a person who is "programmed" by other individuals. He mythologises himself in the same way media discourse mythologised guerrillas across the globe. Jimmy's discourse is structured as part of the idealisation of the guerrilla figure; he aspires to a "programmed" image provided by newspapers and radio. Being granted land for a commune, he does no farming. Pasting revolutionary slogans everywhere, he is swept aside and ignored when a revolution does occur. Jimmy, in his role as anarcho-primitivist rebel is revealed to be a servant of liberal London's political fantasies. His failings are not only his own but reflect the failings of all Western third world idealism, rooted in mythmaking and not in any recognisable material reality.

The potency of mythmaking is presented in *Guerrillas* as the quintessence of political violence. The myth defines who is "terrorist", who "guerrilla", who "freedom fighter". Yet the process of becoming a myth is, for the person wishing to become one, a bitter process subjectively. As Eric Hobsbawm writes in *Bandits*, "to become a public legend a man must have simple outlines. To be a tragic hero everything about him must be pared away, leaving him silhouetted against the horizon" (2003, 138).

We see this in Jimmy's propaganda posters on which he brags; "I'm Nobody's Slave or Stallion, I'm a Warrior and Torch Bearer—Haji James Ahmed" (1976, 104); the "Haji" added to encourage wider mythical association with American Black Nationalism. But what we see *in media res* with Jimmy, we see already concluded with Roche. Roche's guerrilla activities made him a celebrity in London, "an extraordinary person", as Jane describes him, "he had appeared to her as a doer; and none of the people she knew could be considered doers" (1976, 42). It is only when Roche returns to the novel's unnamed Caribbean island with Jane that she realises his hesitancy, his political confusion and lack of direction. The campaign of bombing and sabotage he undertook as a young guerrilla are revealed as the products of misguided adventuring and political inadequacy. Roche reveals as much to an interviewer towards the book's conclusion, admitting "we were amateurs. The situation was different… I'm amazed now at the things we tried to do. I suppose we lived sheltered lives. We exaggerated the effect of a bomb" (1976, 213). Jane's turn away from Roche and towards Jimmy is framed by desire for a potent masculinity; the libidinal factor seemingly underlying both Roche and Jimmy's ostensibly political desires. Boehmer has argued that the British Empire itself stands as a construction of patriarchal posturing, "the expanding colonies had offered the 'mother country' a practice and testing ground for its manhood" (1995, 75). In *Guerrillas*, Naipaul presents the international anti-imperialist struggle in the same light. The ideological signifiers have shifted and yet the silhouette of the heroic young male remains the same.

Naipaul's pessimistic vision of revolutionary politics as futile posturing, very similar to Greene's empty gesture, has led critics like Robert Greenberg to argue that it is "Naipaul's diasporic Indian sensibility and his rejection of black cultural primacy [in which] are found the original of the racial dynamics and antinationalist politics that inform his political novels" (2000, 219). He is presented as a writer who has, following the traditional post-colonial narrative, seen the Empire end only to be replaced by worse dictatorships and hapless indigenous democracies, and, as such, his novels represent disillusion at the postcolonial failure of liberated peoples. His pessimistic tone in interviews helps confirm this: "to be active in politics… is to overestimate the capacity of the animal," he told Fitzroy Frazer in1960, "you cannot commit yourself unless your cause is absolutely pure" (1997, 8). I would argue, however, that reading his defeatism to be a purely postcolonial despair (rather than, say, a general scepticism around commitment) implies a certain British projection. The structure of feeling embedded within the British end of Empire narrative (that of the failure of a great project) frames the reading of the postcolonial situation and what the continuing political turbulence signifies. The reasons behind this can be located within the tactical framework of guerrilla war itself. Robert Taber summarises the guerrilla's function:

> The purpose of the war of national liberation, pitting the feeble resources of a small and primitive nation against the strength of a great, industrial power is not to conquer or terrorise, but to create an intolerable situation for the occupying power or its puppet government. (1977, 91)

British forces were defeated in Palestine and Crete not by the kind of crushing military victory that Castro won over Batista but by a total loss of morale by the colonisers. Prolonged conflict turned British public opinion from initial indignation to repugnance and, finally, overpowered any will to remain whatsoever. Post-war British history is marked by a preponderance of such events. The end of Empire is marked by bitterness and a gut-instinct reaction towards isolationism. On the Caribbean island in *Guerrillas*, however, imperialism does not simply end at the moment of political liberation; the long shadow of Empire's failure hangs over the remaining white characters, sapping their will to continue residing on the island at all. As an uprising shakes the capital towards the end of the novel each of the characters begin to think of the respective Western countries they plan to make a getaway to. A fleet of helicopters rush in overhead "moving in threes, coming down to the airport and almost settling, then whirling away as if angered" (1976, 196). Harry, the store-owner recently granted a Canadian passport, remarks "I was wondering when this was going to happen. The Americans are not going to let anybody here stop them lifting bauxite… The Americans shoot everybody. They're worse than the South Americans" (1976, 196). The seeming "pessimism" of the novel is revealed here not only as a disheartened response to the political systems replacing British colonial rule but the continuation and perpetuation of imperialism through postcolonial structures of capital. The Americans, at once a military presence but also metonymical of the system of global capital, effectively demonstrate the imperviousness of their property claims to the fluctuations and machinations of postcolonial domestic politics. It is the continued domination of developing nations through capital that the end of Empire narrative fails to grasp; something intuitively clear to postcolonial states themselves. The figure of the guerrilla or the terrorist, a representative of ideology and individual commitment at its purest, is here made tragic once again by the misguided focus of their beliefs and struggle. Rather than the horseback riding European adventurer, neo-imperialism's vanguard come dressed in business suits. The terrorists in *Guerrillas* are proven redundant by comparison.

Trash and Terror: The Thriller and International Capital

In Eric Ambler's *The Levanter* we find that the operation of international capital lies at the heart of the narrative. One of the protagonists, Michael Howell, is himself a multinational businessman. *The Levanter* is a text much more confident in British colonial justice than either Naipaul or Greene's novels. As Soraya Anthonius writes in a review appearing in the *Journal of Palestine Studies*, "the whole atmosphere of the book is reminiscent of the era of the Mandatory governments" (1973, 124) rather than the Middle East of the 1970s. Indeed, first published in 1972, the book would go on to become a bestseller following the 1973 Oil Crisis. The narrative develops around three figures: Lewis Prescott, the fearless and rigorously objective journalist, Michael Howell, the multinational businessman educated in Britain whose mastery of business negotiation allows him to keep his private businesses semi-independent within newly-socialised Syria, and Salah Ghaled, a sociopathic Palestinian terrorist who manipulates Howell into working for him. Beside the uncanny replication of the novel's fictional plot in the real attack on Israel in 1978 mentioned earlier in the chapter, there is little to distinguish the novel beside it being what Gregory Orfalea has called "a new plot to the old story of the bad Arab" (1988, 126). It is only when returning to the book with the lessons of Naipaul's novel in mind that the choice of a business executive as the novel's reluctant terrorist protagonist becomes important.

For a thriller novel of only 311 pages, *The Levanter* makes the unusual decision to introduce no elements of tension until 83 pages into the narrative. The first quarter of the novel is given over to an intricate description of the workings of Michael Howell's corporation that manufactures industrial components in Syria. Dr. Hawa, the new Ba'athist regime's Minister for Social Affairs and Commerce, is tasked with nationalising Syria's manufacturing industries in order to move the economy towards centralised planning on the Soviet model. By proving that his multinational connections are indispensible, Howell keeps his business independent and goes on to play an intricate game of cat-and-mouse with Dr. Hawa to secure government contracts and increase output. Ambler spends pages getting lost in the details of supply and demand, the mechanics behind engineering fuses and car batteries. Often this does not even serve as foreshadowing (the terrorist Ghaled uses only a fraction of the business organisation described here for his devious scheme), which begs the question as to what purpose this extended survey serves. Well, as the prologue describes how Ghaled forced Howell to pledge allegiance to his terrorist unit at gunpoint, it can be presumed that this introductory material serves to establish beyond doubt Howell's lack of complicity in terrorism and prepares the reader for the heroic acts he is to undertake later when he undermines Ghaled's plot from within. From this perspective, the business negotiations with Dr. Hawa are comparable to the physical trials undertaken by more traditional protagonists to establish their heroism. Howell's skill at negotiation and engineering know-how (importantly, learned at a British university) demonstrate his superiority to his foreign adversary. His multinational background in transnational enterprise gives his continued operation in the socialist Syrian Arab Republic the heroic quality of an adventure; Ambler reminds the reader often that Howell can leave whenever he chooses to. Ultimately, Ambler's protracted explanation of business practices serves structurally to establish the businessman as a colonialist hero. As Howell uses his keen wits to outmanoeuvre the brutal Ghaled while serving in his terrorist cell, his actions are motivated out of both a hatred of violence and a love of enterprise. The forces he fights against are presented as murderous and cruel, made possible only by "the magic labels 'Palestine' and 'Palestinian' which could transform the most brutish killer into a gallant fighter for freedom" (1973, 66). Ambler's construction of a heroic businessman outwitting socialists and defeating terrorists allows his thriller to recycle the tropes of earlier, more obviously colonialist works by replacing any explicitly nationalist undertones with the liberal narrative of benign capitalist internationalism. Compared with Greene's Catholic vision and Naipaul's pessimism, Ambler's internationalism is unashamedly triumphalist.

To extend this reading one step further, Ambler's 1972 hero reflects values similar to the mercenary protagonist of Britain's best-selling thriller of the 1970s, Fredrick Forsyth's *The Day of the Jackal* (1971). Highly skilled, a master of disguise and infiltration, living the life of a high-class multinational millionaire playboy, the Jackal has all the libidinal appeal of James Bond but without the now-hackneyed premise of servitude and loyalty to the crown. Setting out to assassinate the French President, Charles de Gaulle (a tempting target for the Francophobic British general public, as well as a real-life target of a number of terror attacks), the Jackal's strength lies in his absolute commitment to the profit motive. As his English go-between describes it:

> A professional does not act out of fervour, and is therefore more calm and less likely to make elementary errors. Not being idealistic he is not likely to have second thoughts at the last minute about who else might get hurt in the explosion, or whatever method, and being a professional he has calculated risks to the last contingency. So his chances of success are surer than anyone else. (1973, 51)

The private sector efficiency of the mercenary is also, notably, the reason why the label "terrorist" fits so uncomfortably on him. Forsyth's creation escapes this label in a way that individual terrorists, guerrillas, insurrectionists and even state-sponsored combatants don't. From the emergent neoliberal perspective, the "professional" working for money becomes the opposite of the terrorist acting on ideology, even when that professional is tasked with assassinating a head of state.

The Jackal's multinationalism is not absolutely complete, however. The English reader is provided with clues throughout as to the Jackal's secret Britishness. This Britishness reaches its peak at the climax of the novel where, at the moment just prior to success where (following the standard terrorist morphology) a moment's change of heart foils the culmination of the final plan; it is his national ignorance that betrays him. Centred in the sight of the Jackal's sniper rifle as he awards medals to military dignitaries, de Gaulle "had to bend down to give the traditional kiss of congratulation that is habitual among the French and certain other nations, but which baffles Anglo-Saxons. It was later established that the bullet had passed a fraction of an inch behind the moving head" (1973, 379). The revelation of his "Anglo-Saxon" origins at the moment of failure no doubt served to endear the Jackal to the British reading public.³ In fact, it is this intransigent British insularity in the face of foreign cultures that acts as the focal point of the Jackal's redemption within his terrorist narrative arc. The appeal of the rational and efficient practitioner of business in a postcolonial world is revealed in these closing moments to be ultimately insufficient. The reasonable business-orientated frontage gives way to a British national identity which, on a symbolic level, reveals the objective frontage of global capitalist development to be allied to nationalist expansion. The economic programme seeking to claw back Western dominance following the political losses of the post-war era can in this way be re-encoded as market destiny. The masters of the new borderless world, Forsyth implies, will still be British. The British Empire may have ended, but British business is booming.

Of course, this mentality can be found in terrorist thrillers set in far-off, exotic, former colonies of which a British general readership can be expected to have limited knowledge. As the more ruminative of these novels set outside of Britain have shown, however, looking outwards in the postcolonial moment of the 1970s is very often a substitute for looking inwards. The end of Empire narrative has been formulated in these texts as a bitter renunciation, an exhausted and contemplative defeat, and a cynical recognition of things to come. To continue the analysis of British terrorist novels in the 1970s it therefore makes sense to move on from how Britain imagined its role in the world to how the British nation imagined its own identity. What do terrorist thrillers have to tell us about postcolonial Britain?

Postcolonial Britain and the Rise of Reaction

The process of constructing a domestic terrorist thriller involves an imaginative testing of margins and borders. The terrorist, if they are truly antagonistic, acts in a political space beyond what is accepted as "us", the community, and yet they must also be within that political space to avoid immediate identification and capture. They tend, therefore, to operate on the margins. This book will go on to detail specific communities which serve as terrorist marginalities in 1970s novels: immigrant communities (especially Irish), criminal underworlds, countercultural undergrounds, and destitute aristocrats, among others. Each of these, however, represents a space so far from the imagined centre that it is easy to forget the politically turbulent context of Britain in the 1970s.

The imagined location of the centre is a conflicted and divisive issue in itself. In approaching terrorist novels' depictions of the imagined centre, the state of the nation, the continued application of postcolonial approaches to the texts reveals interesting continuities. Elleke Boehmer has written of how "colonisation was [originally] referred to as at once a metaphoric and a cartographic undertaking. New spaces were interpreted visually and verbally, both as grids and triangulations, and as sentences retracing traveller's routes" (1995, 49). Postcolonial literature contests the initial mappings of the colonists, with "the postcolonial text itself a site of struggle for linguistic control" (Ashcroft et al. 1989, 115). The world maps which put Britain at the centre of a quarter-red globe are long out of date by the 1970s and, over the course of the decade, the meaning of what remained became the site of bitter conflicts. Britain had lost its imperial role and, like an actor, the assignment of a new role for Britain would involve a deep consideration of its character, of what Britain is and what it stands for. Britain tries to discover what its purpose is through the novel form.

Terrorist thrillers, by nature of their populism, map the national imaginary in accessible and unassuming forms. In a sense, texts like *The Honorary Consul*, *Guerrillas*, or even *The Levanter*, provide only one aspect of the end of Empire—namely the sense of renunciation—and so threaten to emphasise this aspect of British nationhood over others. It is essential to understand how, on a fundamental level, British society in the 1970s is ruptured throughout by the failing legacy of the postwar settlement. The Keynesian economics which built the welfare state, massively expanded the economy, advanced technology and provided full employment had, by the late 1960s, overreached themselves and, as a result, the previous consensus between left and right parliamentary parties collapsed into division.[4] High inflation and low productivity struck at the same time Britain was losing its imperial monopolies on export markets. Many former colonies shifted towards purchasing Japanese or American goods rather than their expensive, poor quality British equivalents. That the number and duration of strikes broke records every year of the 1970s did not help to alleviate the impression of Britain as a failing economy (Hyman 1978, 175). Politically, both political parties were in a state of deep division over the proposed European Common Market. These debates foregrounded issues of national identity and sovereignty at a time when immigration from British Commonwealth nations was also adding cultural diversity to metropolitan areas. Immigration Acts became increasingly reactionary; the 1971 Act even including an explicitly racist distinction between white "patrials" and non-white "non-patrials". The obsession with race and nationhood becomes an unpleasant funnel for discontent under difficult economic circumstances. At the tipping point of the crash, the 1973 Oil Crisis, financial collapse was attributed to Arab scheming and, by extension, British weakness in the Middle East. A noxious mix of racial discourse, economics and power politics resulted, empowering reactionary political forces.

Terrorist thrillers responding to the rise of reaction were penned by writers from across the political spectrum. Raymond Williams, the Marxist literary scholar whose work *The Volunteers* (1978) predicted a 1980s where Conservative governments ran roughshod over a non-existent left-wing opposition, makes use of the speculative fiction form in order to leave his terrorists with a clearer enemy. The actual failure of the left in the face of Thatcherism (and the fact that later editions of this novel used images from the 1984–1985 miners' strike on the cover) mean that the speculative aspect to this text is often ignored. The intransigence of 1970s ideological conflicts, rather than the defeats of the 1980s, clearly has a role in inspiring him to write a terrorism-themed novel. The speculative setting betrays Williams' ultimate sense of the present not yet being hopeless. The same cannot be said of novels on right. George Shipway's outwardly pro-fascist novel *The Chilian Club* (1972) suggests, in a comic mode, that a campaign of assassination and bombings leading to military dictatorship might cure Britain of its multitudinous contemporary "ills". In a more balanced manner, Arthur Wise's *Who Killed Enoch Powell?* (1970) attempts a serious consideration of the potential for racism in Britain to lead to a breakdown of order and the installation of a fascist government. It is the question which Wise's novel constantly restates throughout its narrative, "What does it mean to be a Briton in the middle of the twentieth century?" (1970, 134), which will be the focus of the rest of this chapter. In reaction to the terrorist-as-foreigner comes the terrorist-as-nationalist.

A critical point of comparison between the three novels is found in the way they characterise forces resisting the government. Williams' novel, set in a future where the Labour Party—the official channel for left-wing resistance—has been abolished, characterises the remaining left as disparate and diffuse in both groupings and ideology. Looking at the police records of political militants, for example, the protagonist finds "campaigning ecology groups… alongside the Marxist factions and peace campaigns" (1985, 24), the trade unions remain powerful—if unofficial—as does the Communist Party's influence within them, although none of these form the basis for the "Volunteers" terror group at the heart of the novel. Compare this to the targets of the Chilian Club's terrorist wrath and these same stock-types of left wing resistance transform into a seemingly all-powerful alliance of communist stooges. In *The Chilian Club*, the trade unions aren't simply influenced by the Communist Party but secretly directed from Moscow. The activist leader of the Black Muslim League is "a trained professional agitator, Chinese-communist, educate in violence and guerrilla warfare, financed from Peking via Zanzibar and Tangier, a fervid racialist, fanatically anti-white" (1973, 67), later found to be controlled by student activists (also led by Russian agents), given media support by a gay BBC producer (secret Marxist) and funded by a captain of industry secretly radicalised on a trip to Eastern Europe. *The Chilian Club*, conforming to the standard terrorist morphology, is structured by accumulating violence. Each chapter sees the assassination of another secret communist of increasing status and power. At the climax the Prime Minister is revealed to be compromised and, due to a last minute set-back, the Chilian Club accidentally end up setting off a secret government superweapon and blasting Stonehenge "into orbit" (1973, 189). In spite of their plans being foiled in the last moments, the book nevertheless provides a satisfying fascistic conclusion with a military junta seizing power and putting all the strikers back to work. Although the tenor of *The Chilian Club* is tongue-in-cheek, the connections that are made between different forms of resistance (foreshadowing Claire Sterling's work by almost a decade) is not meant to be farcical but quite the opposite. Reviewed in the *Sunday Express*, the connecting of all elements of activism or dissent into a spider's web of Moscow-influenced stooges was praised for its accuracy and the terrorists hailed as "four heroes – and I mean HEROES!" Both *The Chilian Club* and *The Volunteers* share their depiction of lone terrorists standing against a society crippled by ideological domination. In *The Volunteers*, the left is weak and the silent majority struggle beneath a triumphant right wing, hopeless and waiting to be rescued. In *The Chilian Club* the silent majority face the same dilemma, only the forces they are begrudgingly suffering under are an all-powerful left disrupting the efficient working of the economy. The silent majority are implicitly on the terrorists' side in both texts, representing a truer and more natural Britain waiting to be freed from the grip of an alien political structure.

In comparison to these texts, Arthur Wise's *Who Killed Enoch Powell?* presents a more ambivalent and politically ambiguous vision of the British population; one in which the majority are not so much silent as uncertain what to say. The novel begins with the assassination of Powell and takes the form of a detective thriller. Chief Inspector Noel Taylor races against time to stop Monckton, a Machiavellian ex-Colonel, from using the resulting race riots as a platform to launch his fascist government. The novel is formally arranged as a series of short, montage-like sections moving between characters and wider events within the country, providing space for a more nuanced series of speculations about different reactions to the event.[5] The choice of Enoch Powell is indicative of the book's willingness to interrogate national feeling as much as caricature it. Tariq Ali wrote of Powell and his followers in 1972 that:

> The phenomenon of Powellism is slightly different [than pure racism or fascism], as Powell's ambitions transcend the issue of race; he is generally concerned with the creation of a British nationalism which recovers some of the lost potency of British capitalism… he uses racism quite blatantly to challenge the complacency of his own party leadership. (1972, 223)

For Ali, Powell is much more than a reactionary bigot, he represents the skilful manipulations of British imperialism brought home; playing divide-and-rule at one moment to create rupture and division, while rhetorically uniting the divided people under a common cause the next. Wise uses the figure of Powell to demonstrate the efficacy of this tactic in mobilising British national feeling. For the fascist British Union of Activists in the novel the failure of the British people to develop a revolutionary tradition can be blamed on the Empire. A neo-Nazi convert declares that "poverty and squalor and long working hours for little pay are less important to a man than a sense of identity!" (1970, 74). The initial riots are indeed of white working class origin, based around local jealousies and the feeling that non-whites "were stealing their distinction from them" (1970, 34). For the final crisis of the novel, however, Wise sets the ensuing riot at Wimbledon. When a black American wins the final and fails to show the requisite sportsmanship in shaking his defeated opponent's hand, the crowd begins tearing apart the stadium. Wise depicts the destruction as an existential act:

> An impotent fury grew that demanded action. Yet what was the target of that action to be? On what were people to vent their fury? They couldn't

get at Monsy [the American] through a TV set...Then a doubt grew: was it Monsy they really wanted to get their hands on? Wasn't it perhaps something beyond Monsy – Wimbledon itself, or the system Wimbledon represented? Wasn't it really this: Wimbledon projected a London-based middle-class Anglo-Saxon image that Monsy has derided. People clung to the old image too long. Now it was desecrated they wanted to smash the facade. They turned to other images to give a shape to their actions. (1970, 154)

In moments like this, Wise shows a degree of subtlety and illumination in drawing out the consequences of violence on the British national imagination. Where Williams and Shipway frame their fictional silent majorities on political lines (albeit opposed political lines), the role of politics in inciting violent upheaval is mediated in Wise's riot scenes by a persistent concentration upon individuals' sense of meaning and self-worth in the moments before, during and after violent events. Race and nation (the one subsumed under debate of the other in Wise's writing) can be skilfully manipulated by figures like Powell but the underlying emotional crisis of self-definition is a real one, something genuinely felt. In response to the question about twentieth-century Britishness, Wise doesn't offer a narrative in the way the other novels covered in this chapter do. The novel is a very rare example of a terrorist thriller which leaves the political sides at stake in a loosely defined form even as the conflicts between them progress to a climax. It is perhaps for this reason that the "twist" ending falls flat. The assassin is revealed to have been an old Nietzchean philosopher who bombed Powell for using the word "happiness" in a speech and thus deviating from the purity of an ideal superman. The persistent British bobby versus the mad bomber trope goes back to Conrad and, in context, provides a rather phony resolution to a text which throughout has raised many troubling and harsh realities about the extent of British postcolonial turmoil.

Thrills, Spills and Nationhood

The overarching question remains as to how far the form of the terrorist thriller speaks to British national identity in the 1970s and, to a wider extent, how terrorism itself is framed by these national visions and political definitions. As to the first part of that question, it remains clear that—within the popular thriller at least—the terrorist figure remains the political extremist type, the legacy of which is traceable back to late nineteenth century terror fictions like *The Secret Agent* or *The Man Who Was Thursday*. Unlike earlier thrillers of the post-war era, however, the main threat to the British outside of Britain is not due to their own imperial ambitions but rather due to their complicity with the new powers of American and global capital. In terms of threats to Britain itself, the terrorists are almost always from the British Isles. Building upon Katy Fletcher's research we might suggest that foreign threats to Britain are framed as complex and intellectual during the 1970s, with the melodramatic figure of the terrorist relegated to exotic surroundings or, within Britain, to equally exotic political extremities. Where Naipaul and Greene convey the feeling of bitter renunciation behind the end of Empire, texts like Wise's make palpable the anxieties filling this postcolonial vacuum. The terrorist figure is used to express fears of economic and social conflict, a return to nationalist symbols and even the threat of fascism. To a confident nation the terrorist threatens only the death and destruction that they can personally wreak. In a divided nation, by contrast, the terrorist poses a larger threat; that of the pebble which sets off the landslide. Provocation provides the usually immobile populace with the excuse needed to unleash their seething resentments through mass violence. Narratively, this stands as the unspoken assumption underlying all of these narratives and may explain why there is such a preponderance of them in the 1970s. In a less tension-saturated society the assumptions these texts make about the violent potential of the crowd would not be obvious and, as a result, the narrative becomes immediately less plausible were it to be transposed into the contemporary era. It is in this variance that 1970s novels present a useful comparison to trends in contemporary terror novels.

Daniel T. O'Hara's work concerning "event anxiety" is in clear contrast to these 1970s narratives, for example. By contrast, the contemporary terrorist event is framed as a rupture of a normality perceived to be entirely safe:

> Naturally, the present form of anxiety, event anxiety, in its sense of helplessness, does refer to the past, the past of infancy, when we were all helpless, as well as to the subsequent repetitions of such feelings of anxiety. Similarly, anxiety as a prospective signal addresses not only the future but the very idea of becoming itself, as any kind of change or new emergence, and, as such, strongly alludes to the present (and its immediate past) as continuing static conditions that the organism desperately strives

to maintain. Finally, anxiety as a magical safety valve looks forward to or anticipates a future as a return to homeostasis and to a present of mounting excitation, as well as to a past as the repeated run-up to such a present situation…. terror and terrorism now constitute 'a geopolitics of anxiety'. (2007, 64)

For O'Hara, the terrorist event symbolises rupture within a secure present which, being secure, is presumed to persist indefinitely. A rupture of security results in anxiety not only about future ruptures but about the very nature of security itself. Such a reading historically resonates with the 9/11 moment as an unexpected re-emergence of a global threat. Considered in relation to the novels under discussion, however, O'Hara's reading of anxiety appears to refer instead to the continuum. The "event anxiety" of the British terrorist thrillers is part of a continuation of everyday conflicts in overall conditions of turbulence and disruption. The difference between socially secure anxiety and socially insecure anxiety is responsible for the alternate fears of the terrorist: the terrorist as a threat in themselves and the terrorist as a threatening catalyst. Both share the common characteristic of anxious teleology, however, in their apocalyptic visions of a return to homeostasis through violence. From opposing tensions both draw the same emotional expectation; present conditions cannot continue indefinitely, so *something must happen*.

One could argue, on Robert Taber's lines, that it was frustration at seemingly interminable conflict and disruption that led British forces out of Crete, Palestine and other colonies which were judged no longer worthy of contesting. The comparison between colonial and mainland terrorist novels has shown the same structure of feeling to be prevalent in both. A final important point to recognise regarding this issue, however, is mainland Britain's relative lack of exposure to political violence during this period. Anxieties exist, but the framing of terrorist narratives retains the adventurous gloss of James Bond thrillers and earlier exotic tales of Empire. Britain's surprising lack of violence in comparison with almost all developed nations of comparable size during the 1970s (surprising as Britain experienced similar levels of domestic conflict in other areas) accounts for the preponderance of terrorist novels—something which taste dictated against in the Italian years of lead, for example—and the humorous, or at least ludic tone with which these narratives are delivered. A comparison may again be made with the anarchist terror novels of the Edwardian period. Shane McCorristine argues that the ultimate draw of such novels lies in "the idea of re-enchanting the everyday through the anarchist adventures of idle and loafing men" (2012, 43), and that "boredom, idleness, avocation, adventure, and a sense of a synchronous time are all linked together" (2012, 32) to create the illicit "thrill" within these thrillers. In the rut of a stuck time, endless conflict with no momentum and vast resentments, the image of the whole mess being resolved in one apocalyptic venting of emotion provides a certain catharsis; a thrillingly illicit resolution.

Terror novels are always self-validations. Ways to confirm an author's view of the world. The better ones are also negotiations, or investigations, but even the most ambiguous narrative concludes in a satisfying resolution; this is the nature and primary function of the thriller form. To interrogate terrorist thrillers as imaginary resolutions to the real life political contradictions of Britain in the 1970s can only lead us so far. The investigation of form—whether the novel-as-form or the nation-as-form—can only set the parameters of the discussion; the progression of analysis at this point demands an interrogation of particular subject matter. Regarding Britain's list of key concerns when it comes to political violence in the 1970s, the situation in Northern Ireland undoubtedly has to come top.

Notes

1. This image of an international terrorist safehouse in Paris clearly holds imaginative power. It reappears in Steven Spielberg's 2005 film *Munich* inhabited by Mossad agents disguised as FLN, ANC, IRA, and RAF. In a touch of Hollywood lunacy they are forced to share the room with the PLO for the night.
2. The story can be traced in Western media back to Herbert Krosney's (1979) article in *New York Magazine*, "The PLO's Moscow Connection", which foreshadows Sterling's arguments about omnipresent Moscow influence. Israel's Ministry of Foreign Affairs report on the incident lacks a number of significant details which are included in Sterling and Krosney's versions and which, historically, seem to first appear in Ambler's fiction.
3. Despite what was written in the initial 1975 piece in *The Guardian* where "Carlos" was first given the moniker "the Jackal", it emerged in 2010 that the infamous pro-Palestine terrorist was not an avid reader of Forsyth's novel but, rather, a copy was simply present in a room in which he hid some of his weapons (Rose 2010). "Carlos the Jackal", now the most famous name to emerge from the 1970s European terrorist underground,

owes much more to an English journalist's imagination than to the person it referred to.
4. For further details of 1970s economic conditions see Harvey (1990) and Piketty (2014).
5. On a formal level, the novel is incredibly similar to John Sommerfield's novel *May Day* (1936) about the build up to a general strike. Elinor Taylor has convincingly argued the power of the montage form to transform individual events into indicators of mass-level class consciousness and national attitudes (2014, 2018).

BIBLIOGRAPHY

Ali, Tariq. 1972. *The Coming British Revolution*. London: Jonathan Cape.
Allain, Marie-Francoise. 1981. *The Other Man: Conversations with Graham Greene*, trans. Guido Waldman. London: The Bodley Head.
Ambler, Eric. 1973. *The Levanter*. London: Bantam.
Antonius, Soraya. 1973. Fictitious Arabs. *Journal of Palestine Studies* 2 (3): 123–126.
Ashcroft, Bill, Gareth Griffiths, and Helen Tiffin. 1989. *The Empire Writes Back: Theory and Practice in Post-colonial Literatures*. London: Routledge.
Boehmer, Elleke. 1995. *Colonial and Postcolonial Literature*. Oxford: Oxford University Press.
Brennan, Michael G. 2016. *Graham Greene: Political Writer*. London: Palgrave Macmillan.
Burgess, Anthony. 1967. Politics in the Novels of Graham Greene. *Contemporary History* 2 (2): 93–99.
Conrad, Joseph. 1994. *Heart of Darkness*. London: Penguin.
Davies, Nick. 2009. *Flat Earth News*. London: Vintage.
Fleming, Ian. 2012. *Thunderball*. London: Vintage.
Fletcher, Katy. 1987. Evolution of the Modern American Spy Novel. *Journal of Contemporary History* 22 (2): 319–331.
Forsyth, Fredrick. 1973. *The Day of the Jackal*. London: Corgi.
Fraser, Fitzroy. 1997. A Talk with Vidia Naipaul [1960]. In *Conversations with V.S. Naipaul*, ed. Feroza Jussawalla. Jackson: University Press of Mississippi.
Greene, Graham. 1969a. The Man as Pure Lucifer. *Collected Essays*. London: Bodley Head.
———. 1969b. The Marxist Heretic. *Collected Essays*. London: Bodley Head.
———. 2004. *The Honorary Consul*. London: Vintage.
Greenberg, Robert. 2000. Anger and the Alchemy of Literary Method in V.S. Naipaul's Political Fiction: The Case of *The Mimic Men*. *Twentieth Century Literature* 46 (2): 214–237.
Harvey, David. 1990. *The Condition of Postmodernity*. Oxford: Blackwell.

Hobsbawm, Eric. 2003. *Bandits*. London: Abacus.
Hyman, Richard. 1978. *Strikes*. London: Fontana.
Kliman, Andrew. 2012. *The Failure of Capitalist Production*. London: Pluto Press.
Kortenaar, Neil ten. 1990. Writers and Readers, the Written and the Read: V.S. Naipaul and *Guerrillas*. *Contemporary Literature* 31 (3): 324–334.
Krosney, Herbert. 1979. The PLO's Moscow Connection. *New York Magazine*, September 24.
Lakin, Barbara. 1986. Greene's *The Honorary Consul* and Lowry's *Under the Volcano*: A Study in Influence. *South Central Review* 3 (1): 68–77.
McCorristine, Shane. 2012. Ludic Terrorism: The Game of Anarchism in Some Edwardian Fiction. *Studies in the Literary Imagination* 45 (2): 27–46.
Naipaul, V.S. 1976. *Guerrillas*. London: Penguin.
O'Hara, Daniel T. 2007. 'The Cry of Its Occasion': On the Subject of Truth; or, the Terror in Global Terrorism. *Boundary 2* 34 (2): 55–69.
Orfalea, Gregory. 1988. Literary Devolution: The Arab in the Post-World War II Novel in English. *Journal of Palestine Studies* 17 (2): 109–128.
Perrault, Gilles. 1987. *A Man Apart: The Life of Henry Curiel*. London: Zed Books.
Piketty, Thomas. 2014. *Capital in the Twenty-First Century*. London: Belknap Press.
Rose, Steve. 2010. Carlos Director Olivier Assayas on the Terrorist Who Became a Pop Culture Icon. *The Guardian*, October 23.
Rubin, Martin. 1999. *Thrillers*. Cambridge: Cambridge University Press.
Shipway, George. 1973. *The Chilian Club*. London: Mayflower Books.
Sterling, Claire. 1981. *The Terror Network*. London: Holt Rinehart Winston.
Taber, Robert. 1977. *The War of the Flea: Guerrilla Warfare Theory and Practice*. New York: Paladin.
Taylor, Elinor. 2014. 'The Rich Harmonics of Past Time': Memory and Montage in John Sommerfield's *May Day*. *Key Words: A Journal of Cultural Materialism* 12: 60–72.
———. 2018. *The Popular Front Novel in Britain, 1934–1940*. London: Brill.
Williams, Raymond. 1985. *The Volunteers*. London: Hogerth Press.
Wise, Arthur. 1970. *Who Killed Enoch Powell?* London: Harper and Row.
Zahlan, Anne R. 1994. Literary Murder: V.S. Naipaul's *Guerrillas*. *South Atlantic Review* 59 (4): 89–106.

CHAPTER 4

Writing the IRA from the Mainland: Truth and Fiction

WRITING THE CONFLICT: NORTHERN IRISH PERSPECTIVES

Although the British literary response to the conflict in Northern Ireland is of primary concern for this book, simply presenting it without reference to the huge body of literary and historical analysis of the conflict itself would threaten to repeat many of the misunderstandings prevalent in Britain during the 1970s. As will be seen throughout this chapter, writers attempting to engage with the Troubles from across the sea had to negotiate a maze of conflicting narratives which, even for the most sympathetic of observers, represented what could only be described as structural misinformation. Arguably, this misinformation was not intentionally designed by any one organisation but resulted from the collapse of one mode of objectivity—the technocratic discourse favoured during the British consensus years—into a paroxysm of competing partial-discourses. It was impossible to extract objective information from the conflict without mediation, and the mediation of facts was itself a key battleground of the conflict. When British novelists faced this Gordian Knot with a mind to extracting a thrilling narrative, it is understandable why even practiced journalists like Gerald Seymour would resort to caricature. Considering the IRA represented the most urgent and serious terrorist threat to Britain in the 1970s, novels directly engaging with them are few and far between. More common are their fleeting appearances as bomb-wielding extras as in *The Good Terrorist* or *The Family Arsenal*, or simply as bomb-planting *deux ex machina* as in *The Sweets of*

© The Author(s) 2018
J. Darlington, *British Terrorist Novels of the 1970s*,
https://doi.org/10.1007/978-3-319-77896-9_4

Pimlico. We might suggest that the British restraint on this front was due to a belief that associating the IRA with terrorist thriller novels was in bad taste; although the high number of terrorist novels featuring hippies, environmentalists, patriots and colonial liberation movements do not testify to a similar restraint in other areas of publishing. Hopefully, by engaging first with the conflict in Northern Ireland as depicted by those who experienced it first hand, we can then return to British novels featuring the IRA with a clearer eye to fact and fantasy.

Surprisingly or not, Northern Irish fiction on the whole did not stray away from the difficult subject matter of the Troubles even in the midst of conflict. Michael Storey attributes this eagerness to write and read the conflict as part of wider struggles over interpretation which foregrounded narrative as the primary mode of understanding. "The story of the Troubles," as he phrases it, "is co-extensive with the Troubles themselves" (1988, 63). Novels may be serious literary affairs such as *Trinity* (1972) by Leon Uris or *Cal* (1983) by Bernard MacLaverty but could also take the form of the family saga—J.G. Farrel's *Troubles* (1970)—or the teenage romance like Joan Lingard's *The Twelfth Day of July* (1970). Troubles literature sold, and it wasn't long before it started to develop genre conventions of its own. Ronan McDonald describes how literature engaging with the conflict, especially high brow literature, showed a "strong tendency… to seek non-realist modes, to try and reimagine a calcified political condition through a formal restiveness in literature" (2005, 249). The realist tradition became suspect, for McDonald, as "a language which cleaved too closely to surface appearances would reproduce the jaded antagonisms of the conflict" (2005, 249). Where realism aims to better comprehend society through the vivid depiction of normalcy, Northern Irish writers would seek modes that broke up this normalcy, fled from it, or else remade it in more complex ways. Belfast itself, as Laura Pelaschiar writes, became in the 1970s a literary shorthand for "a sort of timeless, ahistorical, apolitical, metaphysical principle of evil, immutable and elemental" (2009, 53). This was especially true for the thrillers which, drawing as much on the history of the genre as the contextual present, reproduced "dangerously asocial, ahistorical and basically conservative" (2009, 55) tropes. The proliferation of the Troubles thriller within Northern Irish culture is a perpetual cause of concern and occasionally despair for Northern Irish literary critics. It was only in the twenty-first century when serious attempts are made to reclaim them academically. Aaron Kelly's *The Thriller and Northern Ireland since 1969* (2005), for example, makes a case for thrillers as a "redemptive transcription" (2005, 56); taking uncomfortable, ambiguous and conflicted histories and reshaping them into clichés the better to be shared and understood.

The use of writing to process, explain and in some cases prolong the conflict is even more evident in the field on non-fiction writing. Reading scholars from the Irish Republic and mainland Britain, one can witness the drastically different interpretations offered when the northern conflict is placed within the contexts of two divergent national historical narratives. In Northern Ireland itself, however, this divergence also plays the role of signifying contemporary allegiances. From the critical opening months of violence in 1969 through to the end of the 1970s one can witness the Ulster Unionists breaking with received notions of Britishness to form a distinct Ulster Protestant identity, for example. Catholic historians similarly signify allegiances through their choice of emphasis; the traditionalism of Éamon De Valera or the socialism of James Connolly as figureheads for the Easter Rising, or the allegiance to the Irish tricolour versus the socialist Starry Plough as flags of a forming nation. Although the majority of historians were presumably not INLA, Official, or Provisional IRA members, the very choice of subject matter, when written in situ, inevitably tied debates to one side or another. As J. Bowyer Bell wrote in 1974, "a new scholarly current can be detected: Irish history is being revised from 1969 backward. The anguish and shame arising from the Northern violence have engendered serious scholarly effort" (1974, 538). Yet, to see these writers as themselves practicing ideologues is to misunderstand the situation. Bell himself emphasises how much of the history written during the Troubles had a pacifist bent, implying that "the real history of Ireland is seen as largely accommodating in political matters, not even focused on separatism" (1974, 538). The too obvious presence of the British Army and the daily practice of the RUC were a living contradiction of these ideals, however, and it was within this context that paramilitary forces of all sides struggled to turn history, like the streets of Derry, into a battleground. "The IRA, since its first effective organiser, Michael Collins, has been textual" (2005, 227), Brendan O'Leary argues, citing the numerous renditions of *The Green Book*—the IRA's manual of urban guerrilla warfare, code of laws and fighting manifesto—as his evidence. Yet the use of writing, and of history more generally, was equally visible in slogans and banners, leaflets and pamphlets, speeches, murals and the patterns of speech and preferred nomenclature within rival communities.

In terms of academic analyses of the conflict, the 1990s saw the most embedded work undertaken in the lead up to and aftermath of the Good Friday Agreement. Tremendous work in the decades since has focused on the still present traumas of the conflict, the forgotten or hidden voices of those who experienced it, as well as the sense of a new Northern Irish identity forming that is distinct from the predominant modes of the past. Alex Houen has written on how "postmodernist policies have been used as a strategy to prevent Irish Nationalists, for example, from contesting the region's 'multi-cultural diversity'" (2002, 243). As Caroline Magennis described in 2010, a new generation of Northern Irish novelists are more likely to position young men as the victims of an old men's conflict than they are to depict the reality of the Troubles; a conflict predominantly between young men (2010, 35). Contemporary academia is doing much to reconnect to a living and diverse history of Northern Irish experience. The same cannot be said for studies during the 1970s. Surveys of academic and non-fiction writing from the era (Storey 1988, 65) indicate the binary tendency between the Irish versions and British versions of events, with the centre ground often dominated by the technocratic analyses of writers like Richard Clutterbuck. The events of the 1970s become flattened out, lacking in specificity in favour of impactful meanings, martyrology or moral panics. Of those "variety of scholars, who bring in their luggage" from foreign universities, as Bowyer Bell describes them:

> The results of the social scientists' interests have been various indeed. A few… committed to a certain Irish perspective, become in effect part of the problem; others drift on to other congenial case studies, uncertain of the value of the Irish experience, but apparently still convinced of the value of their discipline. (1974, 537)

The muddled machinery of social science has managed to carve out some convincing explanations for the conflict in the years since it ended, now that the reality of the situation has faded and the simple, stock explanations presented at the time can be taken at face value. During the 1970s, however, when even the clear-eyed gaze of the journalists struggled to find sense in Ulster's conflicted narratives, academics' claims to superior understanding should be taken with a pinch of salt.

The quintessential conflicted narrative among many is undoubtedly that of Bloody Sunday. The killing of 14 protesters by British soldiers in Derry on the 30 January 1972 has since been admitted by the British government, with Prime Minister David Cameron making a formal apology for the incident in 2011. At the time the Army's false reports of the incident were taken as fact by the British media and much of the international press, alienating the vast majority of Northern Irish Catholics who had access to the domestic press and, with it, numerous eye witness accounts of what actually occurred on the day. There are a number of key dates which frame the Northern Irish conflict during the 1970s—the declaration of Free Derry (1969), the beginning of internment (1971), Operation Motorman (1972), the IRA Mainland Campaign (1973>), the failed truce of 1975, or the SAS's withdrawal (1978)—but it is Bloody Sunday that's shadow was longest, that's interpretations were so totally at odds, and which would become metonymical with the conflict as a whole.

Although armed conflict had returned to Northern Ireland in 1969, this violence was arguably the continuation of pre-existing sectarian unrest albeit at an elevated scale of intensity. The factors sparking conflict ranged from local scuffles with the RUC, to national political turmoil, to the international phenomenon of armed urban guerrilla insurrection and the spreading of its disastrous terrorist philosophy. The Guevara/Debray/Marighella theory of provoking the state into violent action was tragically part-justified in Bloody Sunday. There was state violence as theorised. There was a descent into authoritarian rule too. There was no revolution. The effect of reading about the massacre of protesters, coupled with the British Army, state and press denial, resulted in the radicalisation of thousands of young men, many not yet active in any form of Irish Nationalist movement. Paul D. Kenny estimates the number of Provisional IRA "new members" at somewhere near 3000 (544), a number agreed by Lorenzo Bosi, who also confirmed that those joining had limited "previous political experience [or] involvement in family networks of activism... rather, events of the ground played the key part, more than anything else" (2012, 366). These new members were passionate and politically naive, a dangerous combination, which was made worse by the warrant for violence that the British Army's actions were perceived to have given them. Peter Taylor describes how "if any young men had previously held back because they felt morally uncomfortable about killing, Bloody Sunday removed any lingering restraint" (1998, 126). Once these angry young men (and quite a few women) entered the conflict any pretence to the kinds of carefully ordered and supremely disciplined combat practiced by guerrillas in Cuba or the former British colonies could not be reasonably sustained. The Provisional IRA was its own animal, a phenomenon unique even compared to other separatist movements like ETA in the Basque Country or the Tamil Tigers. The spontaneous armed uprising of a people against their oppressor did not result in new revolutionary forms but quite the opposite; a breakdown of organised resistance into anarchic civil warfare.

Bloody Sunday is of equal importance when considering the British response to the conflict in Northern Ireland, which is, after all, more in keeping with the remit of this book. Where British government responses to increasing tension had previously been dominated by vague handwringing, generalised frustration and the all-pervasive post-colonial malaise, the escalation of violence represented by Bloody Sunday was not something which politicians and the media felt they could continue to ignore. Where those with access to domestic news in Northern Ireland saw the event through eyewitness accounts, Richard Clutterbuck describes how the British public experienced it in a very different, mediatised manner. The protest itself was framed as being anti-Army, where it had in fact been addressing the policy of internment without trial for political prisoners. Rather than a demonstration against domestic policing policies:

> In the [British] public mind the accusations of ill-treatment seemed to be aimed at the soldiers generally, and this, to many people's surprise, brought a strong reaction amongst the British public *in favour* of the army. This was because, night after night on television, soldiers were seen showing almost superhuman restraint in the face of showers of rocks, petrol-bombs, nail-bombs, and insults flung at them by teenagers and elderly women. (1974, 206)

The effect was such that according to a public opinion poll taken in the week following, among British people "who had seen only the actual events on television news ungarnished by analysis, 95% of those questioned considered the rioters to blame and only 5% blamed the army" (1974, 128). Rather than the act of an imperialist aggressor, Bloody Sunday was experienced by the British public as the tragic yet understandable result of radical Irish-Catholic provocation. The false report made by the British Army officers on duty that a gunman shot from the crowd was readily believed by the public perhaps because of this repeated visual priming. The reduction of the Northern Irish conflict in British media to the visually exciting imagery of "aggro" between the Army and local youths had laid a symbolic foundation against which the images of Bloody Sunday were contrasted. The narrative of British soldiers doing their best to maintain order against a rampant minority of extremists fit perfectly with Britain's imperial self-image as benign functionaries and its post-war self-image as governing by consensus. It also established a powerful narrative by which the IRA became the irredeemable terrorist and their British nemeses the upholders of law and civilised values.

Bearing these radically differing interpretations of the same tragic event in mind, we can now address the British terror novels written during the 1970s which in some ways attempted to make literature from this conflict. We can do so now with the benefit of hindsight, with the greater range of insights and historical knowledge than were available to the writers of the time. This valuable work cannot be put aside in our reading, but neither should this become purely an exercise in proving the fallibility of past writers. These novels give us insight into British cultural feeling during the 1970s, into experiences of terrorism which differ in many ways from our own, and, though the techniques of thriller fiction, they help to indicate what thrills and titillation could be found in this turbulent period. We will begin by looking at the most commercially successful novel about the conflict in Northern Ireland written during the 1970s; *Harry's Game* (1975) by Gerald Seymour.

THE VIEW FROM THE OTHER SIDE: PERCEPTION AND PROJECTION IN *HARRY'S GAME*

Now a well-established writer of terrorist thrillers, Gerald Seymour began his writing career as a journalist working for Independent Television News (ITN), the lower-budget but higher-impact competitor to BBC News. His work brought him into close contact with the results of urban guerrilla terrorism first hand, not only in Northern Ireland but across Europe. Seymour's coverage of the Troubles gave him first-hand contact with people experiencing the conflict, both security forces and civilians, while also inculcating him firmly in the media narratives of the time.[1] When looking to *Harry's Game* as a translation of contemporary tensions into entertainment we are therefore already engaging with a text that has origins in partial facts and partial narratives. It is these gaps which the thriller form could exploit for dramatic effect—and it's these dramatic effects which reveal much about the unconscious desires and underlying expectations predominant in Seymour's implied British readership.

The narrative of *Harry's Game* concerns a Special Forces soldier, Harry Brown, who is recruited to act as a secret agent and track down an IRA assassin who killed a Cabinet minister at the novel's opening. Harry is given a backstory as a merchant seaman, Harry McEvoy, who has returned to Northern Ireland in order to join the IRA and fight the English. In fact, Harry uses his recruitment into an IRA hit squad in order to undermine their operations and gather intelligence which, they hope, will lead to the capture of the assassin. During his time he manages, in spite of a lack of knowledge about the local area, to become part of the local Catholic community, fall for an Irish woman, and essentially experience the conflict from both sides. Eventually Harry discovers that the assassin is local IRA killer Billy Downs. However, the IRA themselves have by this point uncovered Harry's identity too. All of this leads to a bloody denouement where the IRA attack Harry, Harry kills Downs in front of his wife, the Army then show up and mistake Harry for an IRA man, shooting at him, Harry escapes, wounded, before finally being killed by Downs' wife in an act of revenge. Harry, we are to presume, had become so emotionally invested in what he saw going on in Belfast that he sacrificed himself rather than withdraw, becoming just another killer himself.

In spite of seeming wildly implausible at times, *Harry's Game* does contain some important narrative points that ground it in the real conflict. The mission is introduced by General Fairbairn early in the novel, suggesting that:

> The problem, sir, is getting inside the areas the IRA dominate. Getting good information that we can trust and can then act on fast enough while the tips are still hot. Now, we can thrash around... and though we may pick up a bit – a few bodies, a few guns, some bomb-making equipment – we're unlikely to get at the real thing. I would hazard the motive behind the killing was to get us to launch massive reprisal raids, cordon streets off, taking house after house to pieces, lock hundreds up. They want us to hammer them and build a new generation of martyrs. (1975, 32)

General Fairbairn, and his author Gerald Seymour, are clearly well-versed in the urban guerrilla playbook, as was the British Army at this time. Although Seymour may not have known it, his solution to this problem—recruiting agents from within the Catholic community to undermine IRA operations—was the same that British intelligence were using as their primary offensive tactic during this period. The memoir of agent Raymond Gilmour, *Dead Ground* (1998), in fact bears a striking resemblance to *Harry's Game* in a number of ways.

The reference to "locking hundreds up", however, is most likely a reference to 1972's Operation Motorman. The areas known as Free Derry and liberated Belfast had been ruled over by the IRA since 1969 independently of RUC control and had become increasingly active producing militants since January's Bloody Sunday. Motorman targeted these areas, mobilising "the largest military effort since the invasion of Suez" (Bowyer Bell 1994, 340) to break the IRA's hold. The aftermath of military invasion also brought with it a change in the legal system in Northern Ireland. The previous policy of internment without trial for political prisoners, established in 1971, had proved not only "a political disaster [but] not particularly effective in military terms either" (Dewar 1997). The new 1973 Emergency Provisions Act (EPA), combined with the Prevention of Terrorism Act 1974, marked the beginning of martial law in Ulster, with military and police powers overlapping and those identified under the category of terrorist falling into a legal limbo. "Defence lawyers," as Ian Cobain writes, "immediately saw that the EPA gave the RUC's interrogators enormous latitude" (2013, 175) and, with latitude, came torture: including MI6's infamous "5 techniques". The RUC would gain a reputation for the acts of torture—real, imagined and real-but-exaggerated—which took place under these Acts and, combined with the use of SAS troops for ambushes, "misleadingly referred to as patrols… to project an impression that these were chance encounters" (Urban 1992, 81), would result in a growing public outcry and a stepping-down of forces in 1978. During the writing of *Harry's Game*, one could argue that the British Army's presence in Northern Ireland was at its most prominent point in the history of the conflict. The use of secret agents at this time demonstrates a keen sense of the real situation, especially considering the daily presence of more spectacular forms of violence on the news. As well as giving British readers a literary device through which to access the otherwise inaccessible world of

Northern Irish Catholic communities, Seymour is also drawing attention to the unique situation in which the conflict placed government authorities. Military actions, of which Motorman was the most dramatic, suspended the *rules* of civilian life in order to restore some of the *conditions* of civilian life. What was dreaded was a collapse into full-scale civil warfare. Secret agents, in our case Harry, are a perfect metonymic device for exploring this situation; their investigative actions place them very close to peacetime police detectives, yet the exceptional circumstances they find themselves in give them extra powers, including an inferred licence to kill.

We know from subsequent testimonies that the real secret agents were recruited from within local communities, sometimes including already-initiated IRA members, but in the case of Harry Brown we are given an outside figure (perhaps even a Protestant judging by his surname) who can bring us into this unknown world with him. We feel his panic when locals ask him for details about old teachers or bands which, should he answer wrong, have the chance of betraying him as an outsider. By the mid-1970s the narrative of *Harry's Game* would have become untenable in the real conditions of Northern Ireland. The Provisional IRA (who are undoubtedly the IRA that feature in the novel), "were restructured into autonomous cells, recruiting members that the security forces didn't know and training them to withstand questioning" (Gilmour 1998, 275). The cell structure, which would become standard operating procedure for terrorist groups in the age of Al Qaida, was a relatively new development of the Provisionals which, without the internet, depended on the close ties provided by community. Not only would Harry the merchant seaman have never been able to enter these cells, the cells themselves would not have had the level of access to the command structure that Harry gains in the novel. The choice of protagonist is effective in dramatic terms, however, and it could be argued that the relative ease by which Harry comes to understand the IRA's chain of command is a substitute for the knowledge that local IRA recruits-turned-informants would have had. For the British audience, the implied authenticity of Harry's voice makes the rest convincing and even thrilling in its revelation of secret power structures.

Yet Harry's outsider experience also allows the novel to indulge in a testing of reader expectation. The mediatisation of the conflict as it reached Britain resulted in two contradictory conceptions of the

IRA in relation to Northern Ireland's Catholic population. The editorial line taken almost unanimously by British news sources followed the government's official line; the IRA were terrorists, radical exceptions, who had used the political situation to their advantage in order to take hostage the majority of Catholics, who were themselves peaceful, law-abiding, and in need of protection by the state. The images of conflict that accompanied these messages however, especially the stone-throwing mobs of kids and women causing "aggro", implied that the Irish Catholics were a people apart, fundamentally in conflict with British values. The IRA is at one moment an organic expression of local feeling, the next a parasite that is alien to the community. *Harry's Game* plays with these expectations, making every pub, every shop, certainly every Irish musical act, into potential sites for IRA recruitment and propaganda. Harry's job in a scrapyard is referred to with jealousy on a number of occasions, drawing attention to the crippling lack of work in Belfast and life on the dole as a cause of crime. In these circumstances, the IRA are always marked out as exceptional; "they would meet together on Saturday nights at the clubs, standing apart from the other young men to discuss in secretive voices" (1975, 89). Among these figures too there were those marked out as "junior officers" and those used as "cannon fodder" (1975, 92). The IRA are clearly embedded in the community, but with each of these descriptions Seymour is inviting us to perceive their brutal, rigorously structured exploitation of that community.

The IRA men themselves present a dual nature to Harry as he integrates with them, moving up the ranks. The more senior he gets, the more "around him [they] removed all but a tight hard core of activists" (1975, 90). The bank robbers, gunrunners and those running the shebeens are shown to follow the orders of the ruthlessly intelligent political men and the sociopathic professional killers. Bill Downs, the novel's antagonist, is notably of the former type. "There were men in the movement... who were said to relish the physical side of killing," Harry describes, "there were stories that they tortured the demented minds of their victims after the kangaroo court... beatings-up, knifings and cigarette burnings" (1975, 142). Downs, by contrast, "was different. Clever. Organised. Against major targets. His feelings were known and respected by the top men. He belonged in the field" (1975, 142). Seymour's prose here becomes noticeably clipped, as efficient in its expression as we are to presume Downs is in his operations. We are to see Downs as a counterpoint to the British secret service, or SAS; a professional soldier, albeit for an unofficial paramilitary outfit. It is tempting to see this calculating antagonist as a projection. The often underhand and devious tactics employed by the British Army, and the excessive policing practiced by the RUC, is framed by antagonists like Downs as a series of tactical plays within traditional warfare: warfare as a conflict of wills between tacticians and soldiers. An asymmetrical conflict between highly trained, well-equipped and specialised state forces and local thugs or idealists would have the potential, on the level of narrative at least, to render the IRA sympathetic. As much as Seymour's attribution of professionalism to IRA senior officers is a sign of respect, it equally operates as a justification for Harry's underhand mission.

The special circumstances of the Northern Irish conflict are also explored in *Harry's Game* through Harry's reminiscences of colonial conflicts. The question of whether or not Ulster was a colonial territory like Mandatory Palestine or Southern Rhodesia, due for liberation, was not only a site of ideological conflict but also irrevocably tied to questions of Irish nationality, history and the question as to whether Irish Catholics were a separate and distinct people. Seymour addresses this issue subtly, never allowing his core characters to speculate on Irish culture's colonial status directly but instead prompting the issue via Harry's colonial reminiscences. "In Mansoura, just out of Sheik Othman, where the gunmen were running around while the boyos in Ulster were still on their iced lollies and sing-songs, it had been so much easier" (1975, 61). He often ruminates on these past conflicts, nostalgic for their ideological simplicity; "terrorists they were then, wog terrorists at that" (1975, 61). Moving into the denouement of the narrative, he thinks again back to "Aden, good old Aden, [where] it had been so much more simple" (1975, 209), and again he depends upon racial delineations when expressing this simplicity; "the enemy clearly defined—Arabs, gollies" (1975, 209). Emerging at moments of stress, these statements can be seen as intentionally ignorant, a pose adopted by Harry as a way of venting his frustrations, projecting the worst elements of his IRA opponents onto racialised caricatures—he condemns the same attitudes when said by other characters, including his CO Davidson, after all. Yet it also points to a sincere discomfort, and resulting frustration, brought about by the terms of the conflict. Having to operate undercover blurs the black-and-white line between terrorist and counterterrorist. He is a soldier in a warzone who can only use a level of force appropriate to the Emergency Provisions Act, while the terrorists with whom he spends every day routinely break the rules of the Geneva Convention. Davidson, by contrast, is a seasoned intelligence officer who has worked undercover operations in Albania, Singapore, "undercover Greeks and Turks in Cyprus" (1975, 164), as well as mainland and Northern Ireland. When Harry sneers at Davidson for lacking feeling, for not appreciating the nuances on the ground, this again could be a projection; Davidson is the authority figure that he must become—someone who can internalise the conflict and make a clear delineation between us and them—yet Harry fails to achieve a similar moral certainty. Trained to see terrorists as monstrous others, "gollies" or "wogs", Harry can't sustain this official categorisation when placed in the field.

Harry's Game ends with a confused bloodbath: Harry killing the Provos, the SAS killing him. Under the narrative momentum typifying the thriller genre there appears to be an inevitability to this conflict and to Harry's own death. The narrative strands tie together such that the considerable discomfort caused by the novel's ideological ambiguities can be purged through the protagonist's personal destruction. He dies in the name of taking a side. In terms of the Northern Irish conflict we might consider this an easy get-out; killing off the main character also kills off the many questions raised by the text. With the conflict still ongoing in 1975 it's very unlikely that a Northern Irish writer could have ended a plot that way. However, it perhaps also reveals the British emotional context wherein terrorist novels like *Harry's Game* found such success. The terrorist novel is caught between wanting to understand a conflict and wanting to resolve it. Every narrative tension that is created by presenting terrorist claims as legitimate arguments has to be paid for through bloody catharsis. For the British reading public of the 1970s, Northern Ireland was one of many interminable conflicts which, seemingly disconnected from everyday life, could inspire a vast array of emotions but never provide closure. The terrorist novel could provide that bang.

BOMBERS IN BLIGHTY: THE IRA AS NARRATIVE DEVICE IN *THE SWEETS OF PIMLICO* (1977) AND *THE FAMILY ARSENAL* (1976)

As mentioned earlier, the majority of British terrorist novels featuring the IRA do not feature them as prominently as *Harry's Game*. Instead, they appear as bit parts or else, in the case of *The Sweets of Pimlico*, merely in the form of narratively expedient bombs. The minimising of the IRA in terrorist novels was grounded in the British media's limited coverage of their aims and objectives. This lack of information limited novelists' capacity to create believable IRA characters. Add to this the widespread disgust that the IRA inspired following their post-1973 Mainland Bombing Campaign and one can understand why, other than exceptions like Gerald Seymour, most novelists lacked the inclination to expend the considerable energies necessary to conduct sympathetic research. As such, the IRA can take strange shapes in these novels. They appear as forces of nature, as embodiments of pure negation, as bumbling stage-Irish, or in forms resembling the Mafia (presumably inspired by the British news' routine description of them as "gangsters, gangs, thugs [and] hooligans" (Barzilay 1977, 15)). This section will address how the IRA became one of a line-up of terroristic bogeymen prominent in the 1970s.

The context for the Mainland Bombing Campaign was the rapid acceleration of the conflict in Northern Ireland following Bloody Sunday and then Operation Motorman. By autumn 1973 Northern Ireland was really, if not technically, under a state of martial law. The law courts retained a degree of separation from the British Army, as did the RUC, but policing increasingly fell to armed combat troops, the SAS mounted ambushes and raids on suspected IRA cells and the Emergency Provisions Act placed limits on civil liberties. After the momentary boost in recruitment caused by Bloody Sunday, the IRA were also now on the back foot. Under these conditions, as Tim Pat Coogan describes:

> Theoreticians like Daithi O'Connell reasoned, regrettably correctly, that the Irish could kill each other off until Tibb's Eve, and even throw a bunch of working-class British soldiers into the deadly stew for good measure, without anyone in England becoming unduly worried – but should a few of the bombs which went up so frequently in Belfast go off in Britain, then the public consciousness would be galvanised – hopefully into action on British withdrawal. (2000, 385)

The prediction that bombs in Britain would turn British public opinion in favour of withdrawal is a presumption straight out of the Marighella urban guerrilla *Mini-Manual*. A tragic delusion of 1970s revolutionary theory. Of course, the opposite happened: support for the British military skyrocketed, and any sympathy for Irish Republicanism dissipated. IRA tactics reacted to this failure by switching from an initial method of spectacular bombing through to a sustained campaign of destructive bombing. The initial 1973 order, according to Martin Dillon, specified that "bombing be restricted to targets at the centre of London" and that "there should be no loss of life to civilians" (1994, 166). The first bombers that would be flown into the capital from Ireland were caught due to the dodgy fake plates they'd installed on their hire car. Once the initial attempt to shock London into submission failed, however, the Mainland Campaign moved out of London—home of an effective counter-terror policing force—to the provinces. They utilised sleeper agents and fellow travellers living permanently in Britain, and mostly targeted government and Army affiliated locations rather than commercial centres. The damage was already done by this point, however, and the impression was made upon the British public that IRA bombs could strike anywhere and, if not explicitly aimed at slaughtering the general public, were at least recklessly cavalier when it came to civilian deaths.

In *The Sweets of Pimlico* the merciless nature of the IRA, referred to only as the "bloody Irish" (1977, 149), is exhibited in two bombings: one in a fancy restaurant, aimed at the diners, and one at the character Dodo's auction house. The bomb at the auction house in particular is presented as "bound to happen some time" (1977, 149) due to the building's precious contents. "English landscapes and Stuart portraits" are seen being engulfed by flames and "smoke poured out of the room where the Veronese was" (1977, 150). The bombers in the novel, never actually seen, have much in common with the anarchist bombers in turn of the century novels like *The Secret Agent*. If their bombs have a target, it is British civilisation and the aristocracy who embody it.

What these bombings allow A.N. Wilson to do on a narrative level is highlight the sophisticated nonchalance of his main characters. The novel is, after all, ostensibly a farce in the tradition of P.G. Wodehouse. It is the story of Evelyn Tradescant, a fashionable young woman whose young lover has abandoned her. Disillusioned with the chic side of London she instead allows herself to be wooed by Theo Gormann—a very old and very rich man, with a dubious background as a "friend of Goebbels"— and his middle-aged, dissolute and bisexual friend Dodo. Through a series of unusual twists and turns she ends up marrying Mr. Gormann, inheriting his vast wealth once he dies and then eloping with Dodo into what, presumably, will be a life of aristocratic decadence. The two bombings have important structural roles to play in the narrative. As such, they don't primarily aim at signifying IRA terrorists as murderous barbarians;

Wilson merely presents them as such in order to show his own main characters' officer class unflappability. The first bomb passes through an early conversation as the opportunity for a joke, "Waiter, there's a bomb in my soup!" (1977, 61), and a segway into a new subject, "Talking of bombs, I gather you were once very interested in Ban the Bomb?" "The CND and all that? No, I can't say I was" (1977, 62). It is during this conversation that Mr. Gormann's lifelong commitment to pacifism is revealed and, with it, an explanation of his Chamberlainesque naivety befriending Goebbels before the war. A failing is revealed as a strength, a negative as a positive, and all of this built on the foundations of an aristocratic good breeding which could witness a bombing and come away undaunted. The second bombing, more dramatic as it involves the destruction of Dodo's business, nevertheless serves a similar function in revealing Dodo's buried heroism:

> Dodo's face became suddenly serious. She noticed a sort of dignity about his appearance which had not been apparent before. She felt unaccountably frightened. Something serious had happened. The secretary has put down her coffee-cup and was looking for guidance to Dodo.... He took her arm, and the secretary's, and was hurrying them out of the office. (1977, 149)

Dodo, until this point presented in the mode of an Oscar Wilde caricature, an over-privileged aristocrat relishing an overabundance of food and sex, is revealed to have a hidden strength of character. In a dangerous situation, it is suggested, the valour of the aristocrat will overcome their dissolute ways. Just as the previous bombing was a turning point in Evelyn and Mr. Gormann's relationship, so this second bombing transforms Dodo into a desirable object for the soon-to-be-bereaved Mrs. Gormann. It also provides the closest thing which *The Sweets of Pimlico* has to a moral which is that without an Empire the British aristocracy has grown decadent and yet, come the critical moment, they will still nevertheless emerge as the nation's natural leaders. As with *The Last of the Country House Murders*, which will be discussed in a later chapter, *The Sweets of Pimlico* manifests the terrorist as the enemy of civilisation; a civilisation of which aristocracy is the living embodiment.

Paul Theroux's *The Family Arsenal* is, by contrast, far more sophisticated in its incorporation of IRA terrorists into its narrative, although they still exist primarily as a narrative function. Theroux, an American writer, uses London as a form of terrorism-therapy for his protagonist, Hood, who takes out his frustrations through pointless terrorist attacks. These attacks are committed across the city in the scaling style of the typical terrorist morphology. Hood is a former American diplomat to Indochina, presented as above the world of crooks, drug addicts and Mafia-like IRA which he encounters, succeeding in creating terrorist plans where their ignorance or short-sightedness has caused them to fail.[2] This brings him into contact with the anarchistic Lady Arrow who believes that "freedom must be taken, snatched if necessary, whatever the cost" (1976, 146) on the model of the turn of the century anarchists. He begins with graffiti, then destructive vandalism, theft, an art heist and aims to conduct a large scale bombing, only to have a change of heart when he realises the corruption and coercion prevalent in the IRA (here described throughout as "the Provos") and ends the novel by destroying their arsenal of weaponry instead. The narrative is a fairly standard one for a British terrorist novel of the 1970s (apart from the American protagonist), but it is notable for its depiction of the IRA as playing a key role in running the London criminal underground. Mayo, a squat-living drug addict and Hood's love interest, plays up her IRA connections early in the novel only for it to be revealed that she is sexually exploited by them; "she's great at entertaining the troops" as the IRA man Sweeney describes it, "a real morale-builder" (1976, 210). Controlling the drugs and illicit weapons trade, the IRA are reluctant to commit violent acts when it goes against their business interests; something Theroux also frames as a form of corruption. The extent to which this is fantasy, or a projection of American conditions onto London, and how much of it is the result of reading the British press is an important question. In terms of readership, the novel was a bestseller in the UK.

If coverage of the Troubles in the 1970s took on, as was said previously, a series of stock forms, with bomb wreckage and "aggro" between youths and soldiers predominating, the 1960s, by comparison, saw some attempts to investigate the situation in more depth. A good example being *Bernadette Devlin* (1969), an hour-long documentary focusing on the eponymous MP's role in the Bogside insurrection, or Free Derry as it was known. By the early 1970s, however, the appearance of the Army meant stringent government controls on mainstream media reporting. Philip Elliot has argued that this was a conspiratorial arrangement between "the army and its political masters [who] worked out a *modus vivendi* with the news media, partly by teaching army officers how to deal with the press... partly by putting pressure on the broadcasting authorities" (1976). It could also be argued, against Elliot's conspiratorial framing, that such constraints are standard practice in an operating theatre of conflict. Either way, the usual sources of counter-narratives, the international press, were so thoroughly intimidated by the fighting that most correspondents "did not go further than the Europa Hotel lounge to meet with officers from the Army's Information Policy unit" (Faligot 1983, 75). Compare the many interviews with local voices in *Bernadette Devlin* with Panorama's *Bandit Country, South Armargh* (1976) and you get a clear sense of the change in tone. By 1976 Panorama interviews only army and police personnel, with British experts and politicians passing comment. Irish voices are reduced to old footage of interviews given in different contexts. The line taken throughout the documentary is also clear: the IRA are not soldiers, they are criminal gangs and terrorists.

Faced with this apparent media blackout, the job of reporting on the other side of the Northern Irish conflict was taken up by the underground press. A product of the 1960s, the underground press was in transition during the 1970s. Where periodicals like *Oz* and *IT* had combined music, drugs, sex and the occult with radical politics, sometimes all on the same page, the 1970s saw underground press organs growing more specialised: *Time Out* for events, *Gandalf's Garden* for psychedelic spiritualism, and, in terms of investigative journalism, the eclectic *Friendz* which became the far more professional *Ink* in 1971. For the outspoken underground, Northern Ireland was already considered "Britain's Vietnam" (Fountain 1988, 135). Reporters often uncritically rejected government reports in favour of the counter-narratives put out by the IRA, or else constructed their own version of events based on left-libertarian theorising. For *Ink*, however, this generalised support of the Catholic population was not so simple. In order to actually get a reporter on the ground they needed to be escorted by Sinn Fein and the publication, as a result, ran its coverage "under an effective banner of support for the Provisional IRA" (1988, 162). Lloyd, the reporter in question, has since described to Nigel Fountain how "there was a bit of freedom in the Republican communities and I was captivated by it, uncritically captivated" (1988, 162). Sinn Fein would use *Ink* as a way to promote itself to young radicals, hippies and anarchists in Britain with an image of a freewheeling libertine rebellion which could not be more opposed to the IRA's actual conservative values.

The image of rockstar Provos promoted by *Ink* would meet its apotheosis in the appearance of one Jim McCann in the office of the paper's editor, Alan Marcuson. As Fountain describes the encounter, McCann was:

> A seemingly irate Irishman who brandished a sawn-off shotgun from beneath his overcoat... with tales of his very own Northern Irish Liberation group, 'Free Belfast', [he] made an immediate and favourable impact on the South African. Free Belfast, he told Marcuson, policed and defended the city... the editor ran the interview verbatim under the heading: 'Interview with a Belfast Fighting Man.' (1988, 135)

Even more appealing to *Ink's* readers than McCann's fictional revolutionary group was his indulgence in drugs, sex and other non-Catholic pastimes. Free Belfast seemed to confirm the idle daydreams of many countercultural theorists who imagined that Irish Republicanism was a revolutionary haven fighting the same forces of conservatism that they were. McCann would shortly after collaborate with Howard Marks running the largest cannabis smuggling operation in British history, using his fake stories of Republican connections to smuggle huge quantities of drugs through Dublin airport, pretending that the crates they were shipped in contained guns for "the struggle" (Marks 1998, 91). Either a psychopath, a brilliant con man, or both, McCann played upon the lack of real information available to the British public in order to sell a radically different view of the IRA as countercultural rebels. It is likely that these misconceptions, plus a general sympathy for those suffering across the channel, allowed more terrorists than just Jim McCann to operate in the squats and communes of the British underground.

Connections between the IRA and the British counterculture would develop for a number of years before being thrust into public eye following the Guildford Pub Bombings of October 1974. The bombing of two pubs popular with off-duty British soldiers was conducted by the Provisional IRA's Active Service Unit, who were eventually arrested in December 1975 after a further campaign of violence. Immediately following the bombings, however, blame was placed on four Irish suspects, known as the "Guildford Four", with loose connections to what Robert Kee describes as "a self-sufficient twilit subculture, housed often in squats and sustained by drugs and petty crime, in which immigrant Irish... played a notable role" (1986, 31). The press would report on the significant support for the Provisional IRA being expressed in these squats, although "the general tenor of such talk appears to have been basically a-political and averse to cruelty and violence" (1986, 32). The confessions of the Four were obtained by torture (McKee and Franey 1988, 426). Nevertheless, the story of the Guildford Pub Bombings would form the basis of a moral panic within the British mainstream media. The counterculture, awash with drugs and long linked to crime, was also now connected to terrorism. The fallout from this panic would result in the passing of the Prevention of Terrorism Acts in November 1974; Britain's first domestic policy permitting the suspension of habeas corpus for terrorism and terrorist groups, and forerunner of contemporary Terrorism Acts. Terrorism had come home, and the hippies were harbouring it.

It is against the backdrop of this media panic that Theroux was writing *The Family Arsenal* (1976). When reconsidered in light of the mainstream media's connection of the Provisional IRA with countercultural squats and drug running operations, we can begin to see where Theroux's unusual presentation of the IRA as a type of London Mafia gang came from. The sexual abuse of Mayo in order to "entertain the troops" ties into already established suspicions about liberated female sexuality, and the belief that the counterculture's promotion of promiscuity had a coercive effect on young and impressionable women. It also makes sense of the character Murf who, in spite of his Irish-sounding name, is a pot-smoking cockney teenager obsessed with spray-painting "Arsenal Rule" everywhere. His inclinations towards terrorism are shown to be based on kicks and "childish" (1976, 47) drug-inspired daydreams. Hood, stepping into this lumpenproletarian mess, finds it easy to take control and channel them towards action, with only the Provos themselves standing in his way; their criminality inspiring their anti-radicalism in the same way that the Italian-American Mafia historically attacked strikers, anti-war demonstrators and other American radical groups. While the real organisational capacity of the Provisional IRA on mainland Britain in fact constituted a mere handful of cells during the 1970s, *The Family Arsenal* draws on the fear of a drug underground to expand this threat to outrageous size. One of course cannot discount the exaggerative tendencies of paranoia here, or the increasing levels of anti-Irish prejudice stirred up by the resurgent British far-right, but there is a particular framework evident here which begins to structure 1970s thinking on terrorism and which the final part of this chapter will address. It is the fear of a terrorist network. Claire Sterling would posit in 1980 that every terrorist cell across the world led back to the Kremlin. We've seen how, in the mid-1970s, the British saw the counterculture as a hiding place for the IRA. In the later 1970s this would adapt and evolve, with a new mythical structure emerging that would link the Provisional IRA to a hidden league of terrorists operating worldwide.

MY ENEMY'S ENEMY: THE PROVISIONAL IRA AND INTERNATIONAL TERROR IN *THE GLORY BOYS* AND *THE GOOD TERRORIST*

Doris Lessing's *The Good Terrorist* was first published in 1985, five years after Claire Sterling's *The Terror Network*, and like Sterling's work it acts as both a summation of the urban guerrilla phenomenon and a fundamental misunderstanding of it. Both texts posit a covert Soviet influence underlying the many disparate terrorist groups of the 1970s. Sterling, former writer for the anti-communist paper *The Reporter*, reached this conclusion by taking CIA propaganda at its word, while Lessing, a disillusioned former Communist Party member, draws on her experiences of the 1930s and 1940s. A naive young radical, Alice, falls down the rabbit-hole of terrorism after moving into a squat, forming a tenants' union, having internecine struggles within the house over ideological purity, leafleting and marching, before eventually letting a Russian agent move in next door and agreeing to hide bombs for the KGB/IRA. "Like a nine-year old girl who has had, perhaps, a bad dream, the poor baby" (1985, 370), Alice is presented by Lessing as following the established narrative path to terrorism through a naive desire to be good, rather than an internal ideological conviction. The special pathos which this lends the narrative is in seeing Alice initially agreeing with the well-presented ideological arguments around her before slowly realising the violent intent which resides beneath the words. Lessing in fact wrote in 1994 how communist dogmas, consciously adopted or otherwise, lay at the heart of countercultural radicalism: "What could be more pleasurable," she asks, "when in one's twenties – the age at which millions of young people have tortured or murdered others in the name of the forward march of mankind—than the excitements of being the only possessors of the truth?" (1994, 427). In the novel, Alice's housemates, an emotionally unstable and politically naive cast of characters, are revealed to be the pawns of professional revolutionaries. These revolutionaries are soldiers with a task to perform, inflexible in their political alignment and unburdened by moral scruples. Alice first realises this when she sees the Russian agent Comrade Mellings' bed. It is hard, unadorned, Spartan; the opposite of the squat which, in the name of revolution, had become a wasteland of decaying rubbish, shattered drumsticks and drug paraphernalia. It is in the fallout from this epiphany that he confronts her over hiding bombs:

> He stood with his eyes narrowed, staring at her, determined to mark her, force her down, with the strength of what he felt. And now this was the man himself, absolutely what he was. She knew this, knew she saw *him*. This was not the smoothie, the conforming spy who had be taught to control every movement, gesture, look; but something beyond that. This was power. Not fantasies of power, little games with it, envy of it, but power itself. He embodied the certitudes of strength, of being utterly and completely in the right. (1985, 305)

Behind the countercultural performance, Comrade Mellings is revealed to be a ruthless authoritarian. This is the point of the standard terrorist morphology described in the first chapter as "The Last Moment", when the protagonist, having committed to terrorism, has a sudden change of heart and abandons the last big job. The crucial difference in Lessing's rendering of the denouement is that the unveiling of Comrade Melling's true personality also inverts the whole process of radicalisation up to that point. *The Good Terrorist* is revealed not to be a novel about good intentions taken to terroristic extremes but about naive young people being led into terrorism by professional terrorists who have been plotting violence all along. Individuals becoming radical are revealed to be the subjects of a radicalisation process. A seemingly organic progression is the work of systematic manipulation all along.

Once we realise that *The Good Terrorist* is not a novel about why people resort to terrorism but about how terrorists actively radicalise recruits, then the presence of the IRA is itself reoriented. The transformation of the squat into an IRA weapons cache only takes place when ordered by the Russian Comrade Mellings. When the naïve young radicals Bert and Jasper go to Ireland earlier in the novel to pledge their support, "They [the IRA] weren't all that interested" (1985, 285). "Who are the IRA to tell us what to do in our own country?" their audience replies "We don't have to ask permission of foreigners" (1985, 285).

Their plans to conduct sympathetic actions on behalf of Irish Republicanism are sufficiently dampened, however. It is only once Comrade Mellings announces that "American revolutionaries depend on this liaison, so that their aid can reach the Irish revolutionaries" (1985, 298) when the IRA reappear and, with them, bombs. Such is the extent that Mellings wishes to impress upon the squatters his ties to the legitimate Republican cause that, in spite of the tacit agreement on his Russian nationality up until this point, he attempts a personal revelation: "I am an American, Gordon O'Leary. Third generation American. An old Irish-American family. Like the Kennedys" (1985, 298). Alice doesn't buy it though, especially not when he tries to pass off the monolingual Russian Comrade Andrew as Irish-American as well. It is only the sound of Irish accents coming from the cache at night which gives any indication that the IRA are even involved in what appears to be an entirely KGB-driven operation. This raises the question: is Lessing presenting the IRA as stooges of the KGB as well, or are they simply in league with each other?

As no direct answer is provided in the text itself we might consider our answer in relation to the politics of the Provisional IRA during this era and the ways in which media narratives distorted it for a British readership. Henry Patterson has argued that although the Provisionals were technically socialist in their official policy—committed to "revolution across the board – to the Socialist Republic," in Rauirí Ó Bradaigh's wording—their real political inclination was almost purely nationalist. The commitment to socialism was a hangover from the policies of the Official IRA and the legacy of James Connolly. According to Patterson, even this commitment to "revolution across the board... defined as the redistribution of wealth, was one developed precisely to counteract the 'extremist' class struggle ideas which... [Cathal] Goulding had attempted to introduce in the 1960s" (1997, 186). The Provisionals stated a commitment to socialism the better to silence discussion on the topic. Any common ground which the Provisional IRA could find with a KGB-led terror network would be on the grounds of tactical convenience and not shared ideology. Equally, as the Official IRA had by the 1970s fallen into a largely reactive position, opposing the terrorist excesses of the Provisionals, it is also unlikely that they would seek political alliances with groups, socialist or not, who were committed to the same urban guerrilla line as their local competition.

In spite of this, according to Martin Dillon, meetings did take place between the Provisional IRA and Hezbollah. These were not orchestrated by Moscow or, as Sterling claims, "funded by Gaddafi" (1981, 289), but were arranged between the groups themselves with the exploration of mutually beneficial agreements in mind. However,

> no agreement was reached because the IRA was not prepared to undertake operations for any other grouping, to be associated with their aim or to become involved in their operations supplying weapons, safe-houses or any kind of practical assistance. (Dillon 1994, 431)

It is likely that, alongside ideological and operational concerns, the IRA's reticence to involve themselves in urban guerrilla alliances had political factors as well. During the 1970s "most of the IRA's cash came from America" (Barzilay 1978, 97) and Hezbollah's primary target at that time was Israel, America's foremost ally in the Middle East. The prospect of Irish Republicans being associated with the death of Israelis, even tangentially, could mean the loss of the organisation's largest revenue stream. As most fundraising in the United States already relied on a certain political naivety among Irish-American donors, the Provisional's representatives in Boston would have a hard time explaining IRA links to the Middle East. As the decade progressed, IRA fundraising efforts were increasingly under pressure from Washington as SDLP lobbyists gained a foothold, convincing influential Irish Catholic sympathisers that violence was not the best way to proceed towards a united Ireland. If a terror network involving the Provos can be said to have existed, its international allegiances were to America and not to the Soviet Union. In 1977, when Jimmy Carter pledged "substantial US aid to economic development in Northern Ireland" should an "acceptable political solution be found" (Arthur and Jeffery 1988, 83), even the seemingly endless funding which Irish-America could provide was proven finite. The idea that Gaddafi, even with his post-1973 oil wealth, could make up this funding shortfall and also support dozens of other terrorist groups around the world, all while simultaneously being manipulated by the Soviet Union, doesn't seem to make any historical sense. The terrorist network theory must then emerge from the idea of terrorists as a force of pure negation. They are both our enemies, so it follows that they are friends.

The possibility of an Irish/Arab terrorist alliance is explored in Gerald Seymour's 1976 novel *The Glory Boys*. The Arab terrorist, Famy, is PLO rather than Hezbollah, but finds common ground with Provisional IRA man McCoy over the planned killing of an Israeli nuclear scientist at a British airport. As the narrative progresses the two men share similar stories of life under occupation and compare their commitments to political violence. It is ultimately this comparison of commitments which places the first shards of doubt in McCoy's mind; doubt that will lead to him turning away from the mission in the last moment and leaving Famy to follow through on their plan alone in a doomed and suicidal attack. The doubt begins when McCoy gets a sense that, in spite of his junior position, Famy is "directing him, controlling him… had outstretched him in commitment…"

> Perhaps it was the hate. He'd heard of it, read about it, the simple hatred the Palestinian hard-men felt for the Israelis, and he knew he couldn't match it. Even in the cage at Long Kesh when he paced beside the interior perimeter wire and watched the camouflaged uniformed soldiers… jeering down at men below, even then he could not hate to the exclusion of all else. (1976, 95)

It is McCoy's very humanity in the face of true terrorism, the hatred attributed to Palestinians, which saves the Israeli scientist's life. Perhaps due to his first hand experience of the Northern Irish conflict, Seymour presents his IRA character as sympathetic. Both are ultimately defeated by an alcoholic British intelligence officer, the hero of the novel who solves the case in the style of a hard-boiled, loose cannon detective. *The Glory Boys*, like the majority of novels covered in this chapter, is a generic thriller after all. Yet it is in the contrasting of Irish Republican terrorist with Palestinian terrorist that a key factor of terror novels overall becomes visible: in spite of the attempt to make terrorism a special and unique crime during the 1970s, there is still a residual tolerance for these ideological others left over from the brighter days of consensus politics. A belief in common ground remains, even if it is slight, and even if it can only be seen when contrasted with a terrorist of a different race who is truly beyond the pale. Terrorists haven't lost their free will in Seymour's two novels in the way that they have in Lessing's. Seymour himself would not retain this approach as his fictional career moved on which suggests that it is something of the era. The IRA, for a short while in British fiction, is still human.

Notes

1. Alongside *Harry's Game* (1975) and *The Glory Boys* (1976), Seymour's 1970s output includes *Kingfisher* (1977), a novel about Jewish terrorists hijacking a Soviet pane, and *Red Fox* (1979), a novel in which a British businessman is kidnapped by a *femme fetale* from the Red Brigades. Although his novels are not literary like Greene's or Naipaul's, they are probably the best terrorist thrillers to come out of the decade.
2. The Vietnam veteran turned terrorist is a common theme among American terrorist novels of the 1970s. Abbey's *The Monkey Wrench Gang* (1975), appearing later in this study features one prominently, and veterans are terrorist protagonists in Thomas Harris' *Black Sunday* (1975) and MacDonald's *The Turner Diaries* (1978). Although such speculation is beyond the range of this book, the repeated presentation of Vietnam War veterans as terrorists in American literature may say a lot about their troubled relationship with that military defeat and the soldiers who took part in it.

Bibliography

Arthur, Paul, and Keith Jeffery. 1988. *Northern Ireland Since 1968*. Oxford: Blackwell.
Barzilay, David. 1977. *The British Army in Ulster*, vol. 2. Belfast: Century Books.
———. 1978. *The British Army in Ulster*, vol. 3. Belfast: Century Books.
Bosi, Lorenzo. 2012. Explaining Pathways to Armed Activism in the Provisional Irish Republican Army, 1969–1972. *Social Science History* 36 (3): 347–390.
Bowyer Bell, J. 1974. The Chroniclers of Violence in Northern Ireland Revisited: The Analysis of Tragedy. *The Review of Politics* 36 (4): 521–543.
———. 1994. *The Irish Troubles*. Dublin: Gill and Macmillan.
Clutterbuck, Richard. 1974. *Protest and the Urban Guerrilla*. New York: Abelard-Schuman.
Cobain, Ian. 2013. *Cruel Britannia: A Secret History of Torture*. London: Portobello Books.
Coogan, Tim Pat. 2000. *The IRA*. London: HarperCollins.
Dewar, Michael. 1997. *The British Army in Northern Ireland*. London: Cassell.
Dillon, Martin. 1994. *25 Years of Terror: The IRA's War Against the British*. London: Bantam.
Elliott, Philip. 1972. Misrepresenting Northern Ireland. *The Irish Times*, September 7.
Faligot, Roger. 1983. *Britain's Military Strategy in Ireland*. London: Zed Press.
Fountain, Nigel. 1988. *Underground: The London Alternative Press, 1969–74*. London: Routledge.

Gilmour, Raymond. 1998. *Dead Ground: Infiltrating the IRA*. London: Warner Books.
Houen, Alex. 2002. *Terrorism and Modern Literature*. Oxford: Oxford University Press.
Kee, Robert. 1986. *Trial and Error: The Maguires, the Guildford Pub Bombings and British Justice*. London: Hamish Hamilton.
Kelly, Aaron. 2005. *The Thriller and Northern Ireland Since 1969*. Aldershot: Ashgate.
Kenny, Paul D. 2010. Structural Integrity and Cohesion in Insurgent Operations: Evidence from Protracted Conflicts in Ireland and Burma. *International Studies Review* 12 (4): 533–555.
Lessing, Doris. 1985. *The Good Terrorist*. London: Jonathan Cape.
———. 1994. Unexamined Mental Attitudes Left Behind by Communism. In *Our Country, Our Culture: The Politics of Political Correctness*, ed. Edith Kurzweil and William Philips. Paris: Partisan Review Press.
Magennis, Caroline. 2010. *Sons of Ulster: Masculinities in the Contemporary Northern Irish Novel*. London: Peter Lang.
Marks, Howard. 1998. *Mr Nice*. London: Vintage.
McDonald, Ronan. 2005. Strategies of Silence: Colonial Strains in Short Stories of the Troubles. *The Yearbook of English Studies* 35: 249–263.
McKee, G., and R. Franey. 1988. *Time Bomb*. London: Bloomsbury.
O'Leary, Brendan. 2005. Mission Accomplished? Looking Back at the IRA. *Field Day Review* 1: 217–246.
Patterson, Henry. 1997. *The Politics of Illusion: A Political History of the IRA*. London: Serif.
Pelaschiar, Laura. 2009. Terrorists and Freedom Fighters in Northern Irish Fiction. *The Irish Review* 40 (41): 52–73.
Seymour, Gerald. 1975. *Harry's Game*. London: Fontana.
———. 1976. *The Glory Boys*. London: Fontana.
———. 2014. *Red Fox*. London: Hodder.
———. 2015. *Kingfisher*. London: Hodder.
Sterling, Claire. 1981. *The Terror Network*. New York: Holt Rinehart Winston.
Storey, Michael. 1988. Postcolonialism and Stories of the Irish Troubles. *New Hibernia Review* 2 (3): 63–77.
Taylor, Peter. 1998. *Provos: The IRA and Sinn Fein*. London: Bloomsbury.
Theroux, Paul. 1976. *The Family Arsenal*. London: Hamish Hamilton.
Urban, Mark. 1992. *Big Boy's Rules: The SAS and the Secret Struggle Against the IRA*. London: Faber.
Wilson, A.N. 1977. *The Sweets of Pimlico*. London: Penguin.

CHAPTER 5

Countercultural Writers and The Angry Brigade

> The Angry Brigade remind me now of those many jazz combos called the All-Stars. Drawn from wildly varying persuasions and directions, All-Stars took on a name and status that seemed to indicate some permanence and common purpose. Having done that and laid down a few performances that were marred only by warring virtuosity they then dispersed back to the fertile ground from whence they came. (Jeff Nuttall 1975c, 52)

This glowing comparison between improvisational musical maestros and Britain's first and only left-wing terrorist organisation is spoken by Snipe, protagonist of Jeff Nuttall's 1975 terrorist novel *Snipe's Spinster*. A broke and drug-addled petty criminal, we are introduced to Snipe as the foundations of his countercultural belief system are crumbling and the heroic 1960s are long over. Wandering through the ideological detritus of his revolution that never happened, Snipe decides to finally attempt with violence what he couldn't achieve through peace and mindfulness; he sets out to assassinate The Man. Even in this last mission, however, Snipe's conscience—in the shape of his inner spinster—gets the better of him, stalling his finger just before he pulls the trigger. Snipe's anger, his support for the Angry Brigade, and his willingness to transform a "revolution in consciousness" into "revolutionary consciousness" using terrorism reflect the feelings of a surprising number of countercultural radicals as the 1960s gave way to the 1970s. The left-wing urban guerrilla of the 1970s became a totem; a living embodiment of the contradictions arising in a revolution grown from prosperity.

Historically speaking, the concept of the urban guerrilla is one uniquely anchored in the 1970s. The literature of the period is keen to draw a wide variety of groups under the banner: Italian Red Brigades, Japanese Red Army, German Baader-Meinhof Gang and Red Army Faction, the Provisional IRA, FLQ in Quebec, Basque separatists ETA, the Palestinian Liberation Organisation, the Uruguayan Tupamaros, the Black Panthers and the Symbionese Liberation Army, to name only a few.[1] Andrew Mack describes how, "what these groups share in common—and this is remarkably little—is a Left rather than a Right ideology of sorts and a belief in the efficacy of violence" (1974, 22). Although another fruitful connection between at least some of these groups can be found in the fundamentally wrong-headed application of revolutionary guerrilla theory. Mack draws attention to Guevara's *foco* theory "developed, fortuitously perhaps, in Cuba and applied, disastrously, in the mountains of Bolivia" (1974, 23). We have seen in the first chapter how the provocation theory falls apart in the majority of conditions and its application in a developed urban setting could be considered absolutely counterproductive if not suicidal. What gave the urban guerrilla tactic its potency, however, was not the calculated praxis favoured by Lenin in the lead up to the Russian revolution, but a more emotional and iconography-driven process identified with symbols—Che, Mao, Ho Chi Minh—and an existential commitment to principle.

The 1970s left-libertarian terror groups, of which the Angry Brigade can be considered the British equivalent, are described by Clutterbuck as "torn by schisms… united only by their hatred of the consumer society and by their determination to destroy it" (1973, 211). Their targets included not only embassies, military bases and wealthy industrialists but also department stores and, in the case of the Angry Brigade, the 1970 Miss World Pageant. The postmodern transformation from terrorism as a tactic to terrorism as a symbol owes a lot to these groups who increasingly celebrated the creation of destructive imagery as a success in itself. Drawn from the aesthetic theories of the Situationist International in Paris, the visceral image is foregrounded as a means of ideological deprogramming, freeing passive consumers from the "spectacle" in which they live. The amorphous forces structuring consumerist society are perceived as a form of sugar-coated fascism. Theodore Roszak's analysis of the post-war consensus as a "technocracy, [levelling] life down to a standard of so-called living that technical expertise can cope with—and then, on that false and exclusive basis, [claiming] an intimidating omnicompetence over us by its monopoly of experts" (1970, 12), poses a target for countercultural creativity to overcome in the 1960s, and for armed struggle to destroy in the 1970s. The comparison between the Angry Brigade and jazz All-Stars is not a fatuous one then, but conceptually precise. Chaotic, vital, and liberated from bourgeois regulations in thought and deed; the urban guerrilla was a walking revolution. One could not find a more appropriate object for the projection of radical fantasies in an age of disillusion and fury. The terrorist still believed on behalf of the rest of us.

It is the bittersweet self-awareness of the terrorist's totemic role that Nuttall captures in the pathos of Snipe's situation. "As peaceful protest failed," he recounts,

> the handful of us who were desperate enough could see quite clearly that the middle-class revulsion that led us to recoil from H-bombs and napalm was the same token that made us ineffectual before the ruthlessness of those people whose ruthlessness we detested. (1975c, 103)

The "desperate" need for the CND marches of the early 1960s and the anti-Vietnam war marches of the late 1960s to culminate in some lasting change, some victory over those in power, is made only more desperate by the "middle class" slowly turning away from the cause. The weight of responsibility left on the shoulders of this "handful" of remaining true believers is a heavy burden. In remaining committed to the revolutionary event the urban guerrilla seeks to inaugurate new events, more dramatic events, more violent events in order to demonstrate to the "middle class" defectors that the struggle continues without them. The desire for acceleration is tinged everywhere with nostalgia:

> In '68 it was pretty good. Pretty marvellous. The high point of the whole thing. Hunter Thompson says he can see the crest of the wave from Las Vegas. The crest of the wave was at Nanterre. Hippies, communists, anarchists, and the French working class, not asking questions but getting on with the job. They had a revolution there beyond Lenin's wildest dreams. They scrawled no cant about bread and potatoes on the walls of Paris. They scrawled poetry. (1975c, 59)

May '68, the impossible moment, demands impossible and opposing responses from the subject simultaneously; it was a complete revolution that is yet to be completed, a success which failed but must succeed again. The event exists in part as a memory of something passed and in part as an inspiration for the future. Caught between both positions, seven years on a cocktail of hope and defeat are intermixed in these "marvellous" memories, provoking reactions which cannot help but be tinged with denial. Deny the possibilities of '68 and you turn away from everything it stood for, but to deny its failure is to ride a wave which has long ago broken. Each response is haunted by its opposite.

The very act of writing *Snipe's Spinster* might be considered a form of exorcism. Nuttall's 1968 work *Bomb Culture* stands as one of the few contemporaneous attempts to capture the Spirit of the Sixties as it happened in Britain. Recounting the experiences of a generation raised in the shadow of the mushroom cloud, stifled through the austerity of the 1950s and finally liberated through CND marches, popular music and the kinds of psychedelic conceptual performance art Nuttall himself pioneered, *Bomb Culture* made sufficiently bold claims for the new youth that the book was debated in Parliament. Yet, by the 1970s Nuttall had all but renounced the movement that he was such a quintessential part of. Talking to Steve Hanson in later years, he recollected how "I belonged to this tradition, helped initiate it, saw in 1972 or so that it had been completely contained by consumer capitalism and now, when I see strains of it... I detest it" (2013, 9). Mired in disgust and disillusion, finding many of his compatriots like Alexander Trocchi incapacitated by drugs, Nuttall left London for a job teaching at Bradford Art College. According to Hanson he still continued his work with The People Show, conducting "happenings" among the unsuspecting populace of the small windswept town of Todmorden. Nuttall's response to the end of the 1960s can perhaps be seen as the equal and opposite of Snipe's. In *Man, Not Man*, Nuttall's conceptual response to *Bomb Culture* published the same year as *Snipe's Spinster*, he makes his own position on the revolutions of '68 clear:

> In '68 the revolution failed. The revolution I mean is the one that sprang directly out of poetic vision. I think it failed because its links were faulty. The link between spiritual awareness and dialectical materialism. The link between spontaneous revolt and guerrilla warfare... I wanted to bring people down to earth to do the fucking job without any loss of sublimity. (1975b, i)

Where Snipe pursues the militant politics of revolt, Nuttall turns his attention entirely in the direction of the aesthetic and the spiritual. The contempt which Nuttall holds in later years for the "dialectical materialism" embedded within 1960s radicalism is perhaps explained by this traumatic severance of the movement into its two halves: the libertarian and the leftist. Snipe, whose ambiguous nostalgias are almost indistinguishable from Nuttall's own, plays the shadow role of the militant which needed purging from Nuttall's ideological imagination through the novel's violent catharsis. This traumatic severance reflects not only Nuttall's personal response to the ending of the 1960s moment, but a series of internal divisions within the counterculture which—traced through the underground press—can be seen to have been tearing itself apart from the very moment the "crest of the wave" broke back in 1968.

The Angry Brigade and the Underground Press

Although this book concerns the novel form primarily, to truly understand the left-wing urban guerrilla as it was understood in the 1970s one has to look to the underground press. Not only a site of sympathetic reportage, the writings and writers of the underground were so embedded within the political and social milieus which urban guerrillas sought to mobilise that the terrorists themselves can be seen as products of the same forces and the same discourse. The heroic iconography of the guerrilla affected by radical writers as part of their anti-establishment style informs the guerrilla's own image of themselves. As we shall see, this shared context is such that members of the Angry Brigade were even contributing to underground periodicals themselves before their arrest in 1971. The same could not be said of novelists. Indeed, during the infamous obscenity trial for the underground periodical *Oz* in 1971, Charles Shaar Murray was quoted as saying that "underground literature is virtually non-existent: Burroughs, Ginsberg and the late Jack Kerouac... maybe in ten year's time we may develop their equal; we certainly haven't got one now" (Palmer 1971, 50). The novelists who wrote about the Angry Brigade did so from without, using them as an inspiration or a symbol, where much of the underground press addressed them as equals.

The celebration of militant politics was not always paramount within underground press periodicals, however. The trajectory follows the distinct pattern of post-'68 disillusion and political embitterment found across the counterculture and even beyond it. A cross-nation analysis of periodical contents conducted by James L. Spates demonstrates the dramatic extent of the shifts. Studying 1403 underground papers from the 1960s and 1896 from the 1970s, all taken from the United States, Britain and Canada, Spates found that whereas "self-expressive" content has declined from 27.8% in the 1960s to 14.8% in the 1970s and "religious/philosophical" content fell from 9.1% to only 1.5%, the space devoted to "political" content rose from 16.1% in the 1960s to 30.6% in the 1970s. Further to Spates' statistical analysis, one can find this shift in content even more dramatically indicated through the shifting fortunes of different papers. Once a common appearance in Britain's largest underground paper, *IT*, essays on psychedelic spirituality, mysticism and Tolkeinesque fantasy are sidelined in the 1970s into specialist publications like *Gandalf's Garden*. Meanwhile, the most popular underground magazine, *Oz*, began to feature revolutionary news, interviews and theoretical essays in every episode from 1971 onwards. An indicative transition occurs in Manchester, where militant political paper *Mole Express* formed in the late 1960s as an angrier version of the countercultural *Grass Eye*. Come 1970, *Grass Eye* was gone and *Mole* was to become the voice of the 1970s for the young radicals of the city. The shift is not just a simple change in attitudes but the kind of internal pulling-apart which we see between Jeff Nuttall and his terrorist protagonist Snipe; the passionate intensity of the political shattering the prior convictions of the dreamers.

All the while the figure of the militant comes further to the fore with their cinematic bravado and stoic commitment in the face of impossible odds. Jerry Rubin, leader of the Yippies and revolutionary prankster, begins his account of late-1960s shenanigans, *Do It!* (1970), with a quotation from the countercultural icon Che Guevara who Rubin had visited in Cuba accompanied by a large group of radical American activists and students. "You North Amerikans are very lucky," Rubin quotes with his idiosyncratic approach to spelling, "You live in the middle of the beast. You are fighting the most important fight of all, in the center of the battle. If I had my wish, I would go back with you to Nath Amerika to fight there. I envy you" (1970, 20). As a piece of propaganda the statement could not work more effectively. Leftists of the first world, idealising third world guerrillas out of a sense of anti-imperialist solidarity, are not only addressed by this heroic figure with respect but actively invited to join him in his revolution. The effect is similar to that of the

White Panthers who, reacting to a flippant remark from Huey P. Newton about white sympathisers needing to form their own party, decided to take him literally. Solidarity with the oppressed becomes romanticisation, romanticisation becomes identification, and identification leads to emulation. The line between reporting on third world struggles and mimicking these struggles is blurred, and not only on the level of doctrine but through the process of mediatisation and image-making in which the discourse is framed.

The implicit questions of authenticity which surround any act of violence conducted on behalf of others are raised doubly when the grounds for violence appear in a mediatised state. In these postmodern circumstances there is a tendency to overcompensate in pursuit of ideological purity. Urban guerrillas sought to disprove the inauthenticity of their struggle through authentic violence. The Angry Brigade can be framed in these terms. Gordon Carr's study *The Angry Brigade* (2010) frames their campaign of vandalism and bombing against British property between 1970 and 1972 as the logical end result of a leftier-than-thou culture which emerged on the fringes of radical libertarianism:

> To the new libertarian, the revolution was now a continuing and growing process. They dismissed the International Socialists, the International Marxist Group, the Workers Revolutionary Party, all the Trotskyist-based groups, as far too authoritarian, more concerned with building political parties than in developing political consciousness. These elitists [were] substituting one kind of political oppression for another. (2010, 43)

In the place of Marxist organisation, the Angry Brigade favoured the Bakhuninist approach of pure dismantling or, as Angry Brigade contemporary and one-time suspected member Stuart Christie described it in 1970, "opening the floodgates of anarchy". Their targets, outlined in their first communiqué, appearing in *IT* in 1970, included "Embassies, High Pigs, Spectacles, Judges, [and] Property" (Carr 2010, 238).

Central to the pursuit of these aims was the need for constant reassurance and re-commitment to the principle of violent revolution. Interviewed in *Mole Express* No. 27, they phrase the process in these terms: "revolutionary consciousness is feeling ourselves to be in a state of war with the capitalist state every day" (1971, 12). This "consciousness" is not that of Lukacs or Gramsci, an organic ideology emerging from the actual conditions of proletarian life, but a conscious construction at lived variance with the world. Reading the prison letters of Ian Purdie the comparisons between this "revolutionary consciousness" and the wilful psychedelic constructions of the counterculture are subtly visible:

> Ultimately we are making a frontal attack on their ideology. It has to be part of our strategy to let a jury see that we are not attacking any interest but that of the exploiter and we seek to better the quality of everyday life. I'm reading Sorel and there's a little dictum that spins through my head making me giddy and kind of proud: 'Socialists must be convinced that the work to which they are devoting themselves is a serious formidable and sublime work': recognising that the revolution isn't based merely on the industrial front it's just one of those small things that gives you more strength. (1971, 5)

Appearing in *IT* issue 111, opposite news of the Angry Brigade bombing of a Territorial Army depot, this "formidable and sublime" vision is framed by its destructive, if underwhelming, reality. The Angry Brigade's explosives never approached the level of the Italian Red Brigades or the Baader-Meinhof Band, doing very little damage and arguably acting more symbolically than militarily. The effectiveness of the group was to be measured in terms of its actions' semiological meanings.

With this in mind, Robert Dickinson's discovery in *Imprinting the Sticks* that Angry Brigade members Chris Bott and Hilary Creek themselves contributed to underground periodical *Mole Express*, numbers 12 and 13, brings home the close relationship between these left-wing terrorists and the counterculture they emerged from. Dickinson comments on how,

> While the underground as a structure may have been torn apart [by how they responded to the Angry Brigade's trial in 1972], the Angry Brigade episode also represents a gathering together of several intellectual strands which the British counterculture had experimented and played with... the Angry Brigade brand of situationism was peculiarly English. (1997, 65)

The bombing as a symbol of resistance, even of hopeless and futile resistance, may not convert many outsiders to the Brigade's cause but its cathartic power was one which tied into the same undercurrents of alienation and persecution fuelling radicalism across the English counterculture. Reading the Brigade's contributions to *Mole Express* no. 12 their voice is an inclusive one, communicating directly to *Mole*'s like-minded readership behind the guise of anonymity. "TOGETHER," they write, "we must resist their swoops and snoops into our homes and lives or else more individuals will be picked off, innocent or guilty and their efforts will split and separate OUR movement" (1970, 4). The same issue also includes anonymous contributions from inside the Mersey tunnel construction, Chorlton Police Office, Manchester Press Office and one from "A pissed off BSC [British Steel Corporation] Employee" (1970, 8). The community of fellow travellers evidenced in the polyphony of voices within *Mole Express*, a relatively small regional paper by underground press standards, is indicative of the structures of feeling and networks of communication out of which the Angry Brigade emerged.

The position taken by the British libertarian-left of the 1970s against "the system" at large was taken partly in response to the excesses of the state itself, most notably the police. The Angry Brigade's anonymous piece on themselves in *Mole Express* sits opposite a report of a suspected petrol bomber in custody "threatened—at one stage with an unspecified 'water torture'—and, unless one believes police denials—physically attacked [including being] spread-eagled on the floor as cops trod on his hands and feet" (1970, 3). The institutionalised violence of the police has since been well documented, with the excesses of Greater Manchester's force during the 1960s and 1970s being responsible, according to C.P. Lee, for the "shut down of a thriving arena of cultural practices" (2002, 83) across the city. Activities as innocuous as drinking in pubs past the 9:30 p.m. legally-established closing time. The Misuse of Drugs Act, 1971 held property owners legally responsible for any narcotics found on their premises, effectively shutting down the music scene. As with Arthur Marwick's diagnosis of May '68 as a backlash against authoritarian police tactics, the alliance of bohemian and proletarian in the underground could easily be read as a response to the Puritanical excesses of the police.

It was not only *Mole Express* who claimed that "None of us are Free while our [Angry Brigade] Brothers and Sisters are in Jail", as a headline from issue no. 27 put it. *Oz* 37 saw the case against the bombers as undeniably a miscarriage of justice as:

> if you have long hair, if you're the wrong colour or a woman or gay, if you are a worker going on strike or if you are a kid just trying to stop getting bored, you're likely to get the same treatment. Anyone who is ANGRY will get the same treatment. (1971b, 9)

IT drew parallels between the trial of the Angry Brigade and the excessive new Criminal Damages Act being brought into law seemingly in response to the group. The Act proposed ten year sentences and limitless fines for damaging property; "the underground press, unofficial strikers, blacks [and] dopers are all under attack... if that doesn't amount to a declaration of war on the far out freaky left, nothing does" (1971a, 10). When 600 people marched to Holloway prison in solidarity with the newly sentenced terrorists, an action unimaginable in our contemporary situation, one can see behind it the apparatus of social control and persecution which led to this position (Wilbur 1972). In describing Baader-Meinhof's lingering appeal within German literature, Julian Preece writes of how the group "accrues so many religious and mythological meanings when transferred to literature" (2012, 166). The relatively limited responses to the Angry Brigade, partly due to its comparatively benign status as minor national threat, may also be attributable to the overwhelming number of concerns they shared with the rest of the population. The conspiratorial and polarised Britain of the 1970s took more sympathy on these terrorists than could be imagined in any contemporary circumstance.

THEORY, SPECTACLES, DRAMA AND ODDITY

One might also find in the Angry Brigade's lack of impact an indicator of the little known status of critical theory in Britain compared to its burgeoning success across the channel. Simon During has commented that "the Anglophone world nurtured no post-Leninist theorist of its own; no Althusser, no Foucault, no Derrida... theory with that kind of authority requires a philosophical tradition lacking... in Britain" (2007, 36). The pragmatic tendency in British intellectual writing was inspiring its own post-1956 New Left—writers like Stuart Hall, Raymond Williams, E.P. Thompson and Richard Hoggart—who were never likely to justify violence or write anything which tacitly might. Looking to some of the most influential figures in contemporary continental theory, on the other hand, and guerrilla connections emerge in a surprising number of places. Felix Guattari ran suitcases of money across France for the FLN. Antonio Negri was arrested after the assassination of Aldo Moro by the Red Brigades and his journal *Potere Operaio* (Worker's Power) was considered their chief ideological mouthpiece. Alain Badiou, although not connected directly to terrorist groups, spent the late 1960s and 1970s in increasingly more militant Maoist groups such as the UCFml, singing the unquestioning praise of the Chinese cultural revolution. Although, under the poststructuralist rules created by these very thinkers, the biography of the author should imply no judgement of their work, historically these details indicate how continental theory was at once more radical, more popular and, importantly, more catalytic than its British counterpart. The intellectuals of the continent were often more forceful in their calls to action than the most militant of British trade unions.

The one branch of theory that did make some visible impact in British creative circles (if not within the academy itself) was Situationism. When the Angry Brigade targeted "Spectacles" in their first communiqué it was in direct reference to Guy Debord's *Society of the Spectacle*, first published in English in 1970. Debord diagnosed the mediatised society of late capitalism as one regulated by images; the omnipresent "spectacle" which the consumer passively internalises. Against this tidal wave of images, the Situationists launched counter-images, *détournements*, to invert capitalism against itself and shake individuals out of the spectacle's hold. Perhaps overstated, the creative forms emerging from the insurrection of May '68 are often attributed to this theory. As Alex Houen writes, it also has a tendency to recur within the theoretical frameworks and justifications of left-libertarian terror groups. "The theatricality of situations work against the spectacle's separating effects," he writes, "eliciting a free interaction of elements within an environment. This is how a new mode of political violence emerges" (2001, 201). When "violence" is theorised out of meaningful existence (language itself is a form of violence, etc.) the difference between a subversive artwork and a bomb becomes increasingly difficult to discern. In less theoretical terms, the argument for terrorism "waking up" a population appears even in Robert Taber's *War of the Flea*:

> Limitations that were formerly accepted all at once become intolerable. The hint of imminent change suggests opportunities that had not been glimpsed until now. The *will to act* is born. It is as though people everywhere were saying: *Look, here is something we can do, or have, or be, simply by acting. Then what have we been waiting for? Let us act!* (1970, 19, emphases in original)

The sub-Nietzschean privileging of the "will to act" on which this theory depends ties Taber's comments back to those of Ian Purdie reading Sorel in his prison cell. The conflation of aesthetics and violence as comparable means of forcing epiphanies, sublime realisations, from a passive public demands a conscious effort from the terrorist. "Consciousness" of purpose can overcome the "unconscious" cycles of everyday life.

One of the very few British Situationists, Alexander Trocchi, made his own plans for such a revolution in consciousness. His "Invisible Insurrection of a Million Minds" known as Project Sigma aimed to bring together writers from across creative, medical and political fields in the hope that their collective contributions to the Sigma might do to British society what Trotsky did to Russia at the outbreak of revolution; beginning by "seizing the communications" (1991, 186). Held in the John Rylands archive in Manchester, the membership list of Project Sigma includes some interesting and unexpected names. Alongside Trocchi's known friends and collaborators such as William Burroughs, John Cage, Guy Debord and Jeff Nuttall, the names of Norman Mailer, Anthony Burgess, Joan Littlewood and R.D. Laing make appearances.[2] Laing, innovative psychotherapist and champion of the anti-psychiatry movement, even contributed a series of articles for inclusion in a Sigma document. Although the final document was not forthcoming due to Trocchi's personal problems, Laing's own 1967 work *The Politics of Experience and the Bird of Paradise* demonstrates a willingness to align his own ideas concerning mental health and society into a broader aesthetic and revolutionary project for freeing "consciousness":

> All those who seek to control the behaviour of large numbers of other people work on the *experiences* of those other people. Once people can be induced to experience a situation in a similar way, they can be expected to behave in similar ways. Induce people all to want the same things, hate the same things, feel the same threat, then their behaviour is already captive. (1981, 80)

From all sides the work of de-programming a brainwashed society acted on by malignant forces was on the agenda. The Angry Brigade might be considered at the far political end of this sliding scale, were the scale not so diverse as to have multiple, misaligning and overlapping ends.

In direct comparison with the libertarian-left bomber seeking to shatter the spectacle through violence one finds the far more benign figure of the performance artist. Both emerge into public visibility after 1968 and both seek to break down the hold of the spectacle upon the consumer society. Both were also highly theoretically conscious in their approaches—Peter Ansorge's review of the first five years of experimental theatre is entitled *Disrupting the Spectacle* (1975). The term which came to define the new and provocative forms of public theatre pioneered by these dramatists was the "happening". Described by Jinnie Schiele:

> This type of event, often interrupting another, challenged an audience's preconceptions about the nature of theatre. The audience was provoked into playing a positive role in the proceedings; in the process its role as spectator and the actor's role as communicator were redefined. (2005, 194)

The happening is a break, an "interruption" of the steady flow of images comprising the spectacle, forcing the public out of their role as passive spectator and into a new, more vital role as active agent, participant and collaborator, or else as antagonist and disruptor of the dramatists' own disruptions. The very form of the happening engages in a revolutionary refiguring of subjectivities keeping with Situationist theory. Some pieces were satirical in their political targets; Jerry Rubin's bid to get a pig elected U.S. President, for instance. Some, however, were more opaque and challenging in their provocations. Among these we can count Jeff Nuttall's own work with The People Show which he pioneered back in the early 1960s, long before the term "happening" had been conjured as a way of describing (and pigeonholing) his pieces.

In 1968's *Bomb Culture*, it is to the powers of provocation and spectacle-shattering which Nuttall submits the future of all art and creativity. Commitment to the creative act, even the smallest and least appreciated instance, builds momentum as part of a mass underground movement in consciousness-raising. Like the Angry Brigade who machine-gunned the Spanish embassy only for the minimal damage to go undiscovered for a week, the action acts as much upon the actor as the one acted upon:

> These are not stunts whose purpose is to attract public attention; they are ends in themselves. Each event, poster, whatever, should spread like a rash: identification with other people, a sense of the common condition of humanity, disgust and alarm at the political situation, a love of the life principle and each other, above all the direct awareness of flesh and spirit, a proper and fully realised sense of self. (1968, 186)

The "rash" of revolutionary consciousness is, now allied with the aesthetic principles of awareness, honesty and directness in the act of creativity and being. The importance of the movement from private to public space is central in these terms. Nuttall's first provocations, beginning with "People Show Number One" in 1966, took place in the basement of high brow bookshop Better Books to a select crowd of willing participants. A letter from fellow conceptual artist and activist, Mike Kurstow, in November 1967 clearly indicates the evolution of their aesthetics from staged performance to visceral imposition of drama into life:

> Out of my experience travelling around London in the past few months, I'd say that the major problem is this: how to find those situations in which your poem/song/painting/sculpture/event GET INSERTED INTO EVERYDAY LIFE. We're got to discover structures and platforms that can intrude into those occasions where people come together naturally.... Only one rule for the whole thing; we've got to be effective and strike where it works, and never never never congratulate ourselves on our own audacity.

From the conspiratorial insurrectionary network of Trocchi's Project Sigma to the development of public performance art, the mode by which the radical art and writing of the late 1960s is framed here bears great resemblance to the urban guerrilla groups theorising of the 1970s. The effective "strike", couched in combat terms, which one must undertake with a martial professionalism, unflinching, "never congratulating ourselves" but always moving forward. The "everyday life" into which they seek to insert their images, performances and writing acts as a site of both disruption and immersion: one is reminded of Mao's fish-like guerrilla for whom the people are a river. And, as with Mao, national tradition played a key role in revolutionary subversion. Actions almost always took the form of an inversion of Britishness. A red, double-decker London bus was converted into a macabre obstacle course. *Detourned* ads for British produce were pasted on the underground or else given away in the form of free morning papers. Captured on the cover of Nuttall's *Performance Art, Volume 2: Scripts* (1979), The People Show performed acts of S&M while dressed in bowler hats and yell poetry through a loudhailer as the general public line the riverbank looking on. The euphemism and prudery upon which British manners are built, and with it its class structure, are confronted by the private in the midst of the public, the unconscious invading the ordered, the obscene infecting the daily routine "like a rash".

Jeff Nuttall continued his performance art long into the 1970s, albeit with an ever-reducing number of fellow performers. The great split which *Snipe's Spinster* represents in his post-1960s thinking is not only a break with the political, but also with the great bugbear of the underground: drugs. The association of drugs and militant politics in Nuttall's mind after his disillusion with the 1960s "movement" can be read in his response to a letter from a former colleague in March 1975. Released from prison after serving time for drug offences, the writer accuses Nuttall of celebrating drugs as a way of "blackmailing people into slave labour", of libelling him in *Bomb Culture* and of abandoning his former commitments. In a rather curt response, Nuttall dismissed his allegations and wrote:

> I would suggest that the real reason you went to jail and hospital and I didn't is not because of my book but because you went deeply into dope and I didn't.... Didn't you ridicule me on at least two occasions for my cowardice (good sense now) and timorousness about drugs (I had seen day by day that Trocchi goodn't [sic] organise himself to take a shit and my own articulacy was suffering from the modest amounts of speed I – er – dropped?) (1975a)

Having forcefully made his position clear, Nuttall ends on the note that "I've just written a book called 'Snipe's Spinster' which should cut me off from the whole disaster. No you're not in it" (1975a). The role of drugs, like the role of the urban guerrilla in the iconography of the underground press, is rife with machismo and competitive posturing. Nuttall's often brutal commitment to showing life at its most vital and unmediated, his focus on communication and audience response in his work, is ultimately opposed to the narcotic and solipsistic drug experience. In a moment of clarity, Snipe very clearly associates the drug phenomenon with the forces of militarism and imperialism he is setting out to oppose and destroy:

> The fuel of these processes was always there, not so much acid as the Vietnam war and heroin, the incredibly vicious facts of life in the American heroin market. Veterans returning to Mom and Apple Pie after countless Mai Lai atrocities had accustomed themselves to butchery as a day-to-day

commonplace to such an extent that murder was an easy thing to have recourse to on Main Street. In any case, most of them had cushioned their shock and terror by experiencing it through the oceanic tides of pot and heroin... confusing the atrocity with hallucinatory nightmares and relegating both to a distanced category of insignificance. (1975c, 108)

The political murderer, like the murderer acting on behalf of drug dealers, is simply an inversion of larger capitalist power dynamics. The drug is the consumable commodity which clouds this materiality and gives it the sensation of a pure spectacle. Eric Mottram, writing in an 11-page analysis of *Snipe's Spinster* which he sent to Nuttall, places this paradoxical position of the libertarian-left at the heart of the novel, suggesting that "certainly the killing is a superego action; orders from above, as Burroughs would say... LSD and a haircut do not a revolution make" (1975). The "superego action", as an internalisation of the Name of the Father, is the imposition of moral orders above the actions of the ego. Marcuse had already indicated in *Eros and Civilisation* how post-industrial capitalism's tendency towards "repressive desublimation" allies the narcotic release of drugs and libertinism with the traditional prescriptive repressions of the industrial stage. Snipe oscillates between the narcotically fortified imperative to assassinate and the socially conformist demands of his inner Spinster. Rather than the unmediated experience Nuttall sought from his performances, Snipe is engaged in a deeply structured battle of wills between two ideologically determined poles.

The final message of *Snipe's Spinster* is summarised by Mottram in existential terms; "carrying a bomb may or [may] not have political meaning beyond the need to act somehow, but it certainly may give the kick which is the drug of the energy addict... what all these vitalist figures and groups require is alibis" (1975). The ultra-left celebration of revolution as vitality and commitment seeks to exorcise the oppressed/oppressor roles which all external power results in. In the end, however, it inevitably ends up internalising power structures and oppressions in the quest to purify and idealise the self. A parallel can be drawn here with Angela Carter's 1972 terrorism-themed novel *The Infernal Desire Machines of Doctor Hoffman*. By developing a machine which gives desires corporeal forms Dr Hoffman removes the material basis of the world. The resulting libidinal freedom bears close resemblance to a fascist dictatorship wherein power and sexuality determine existence for their own sake. The primacy of the will transforms all relations into sadomasochisms. The footsoldiers leading this revolution in consciousness are described as "amorphous spooks... Dr Hoffman's guerrillas, his soldiers in disguise who, though absolutely unreal, nevertheless, were" (1982, 12). They are creatures of pure will and vision which exist beyond the world's real material conditions. As Nuttall does with Snipe, Carter reveals through her interaction with political violence a deep scepticism about both libidinal freedom and dogmatic extremism. Both modes of being are seen to inevitably collapse into each other within the idealist void, denying the material world they would seek to change.

SYMPATHY WITH THE REBEL: TERRORIST AS CIPHER IN *THE ANGRY BRIGADE* (1973) AND *CHRISTIE MALRY'S OWN DOUBLE-ENTRY* (1973)

Jeff Nuttall's closeness to the underground and the British counterculture has made him an ideal reference point for our discussion of the Angry Brigade so far. It was not only writers sharing the Angry Brigade's milieu who took them as literary inspiration, however. Writers socially detached from the world of squats and psychedelic drugs still found in the Angry Brigade a potent set of symbols through which to think their own relation with society and the capitalist system. Two of these writers, B.S. Johnson and Alan Burns, turn to writing terrorist novels in the early 1970s out of a different set of disillusions than those lamenting the "broken wave" of '68. Experimental novelists, their attitude to the counterculture was dismissive at best (Johnson sued the *Daily Mail* for libel after they called him a "hippy"). Both, nevertheless, joined anti-Vietnam demonstrations and pressured the Arts Council to improve pay and conditions for writers, especially those doing something different, or "writing as though it mattered" (1973) to use Johnson's phrasing. It wasn't until the 1970 Industrial Relations Bill, however, that they found a cause they could devote their full time and energies to. The writers collaborated on two short films made for the ACTT union, *March!* (1970) and *Unfair!* (1970). Made to be travelled around the country and projected on factory walls during lunch breaks, Johnson remarked to Burns in a 1973 interview his contentment that such films "helped a bit in mobilising the trade union movement" (1981, 89). Johnson also used his public platform to write a number of articles on the proposed Bill and how, without a strong enough mobilisation of the trade unions against it, the rights of workers hard won over the course of generations would be stripped away in a moment. In spite of this commitment, and the commitment of many in unions across the country, the Bill passed into law in 1971.[3] It is against this disappointment that the disillusion of these writers can be witnessed, rather than the failings of the '68 moment. The result, however, is the same as that of Nuttall's journey; the choice of the Angry Brigade as a useful literary cipher for the expression of political frustrations and existential angst.

Alan Burns' 1973 novel is more obviously a reflection on the group; its title being *The Angry Brigade* and its subject matter being a fictional account of a commune's radicalisation. Of the two authors, Burns's oeuvre is also the closest to the kinds of vitalist, quasi-Situationist work being produced by Nuttall and others in experimental theatre. In 1970 he collaborated with fringe theatre producer Charles Marowitz on another fictionalisation of a real-life, extreme political gesture in *Palach*, an experimental play concerning the life of Jan Palach. Palach's self-immolation was considered a protest against the failure of the Prague Spring in 1968. The failure of Czechoslovakia to break away from the Soviet Union only exists in the background of the play. Historical events are presented through audio recordings, news-clippings and statements from the Communist Party. It is Palach's inability to break away from his family who, in turn, are incapable of breaking out of their daily routines (even in the midst of an uprising) which seem to drive him to his act. The act itself is implied through audio as many different statements, readings, songs and sound effects are blasted through the speakers surrounding the audience. The sound of 1970s valve amplifiers pushed to such extremes would create electronic distortion effects reminiscent of burning and high-pitched screaming, as well as being physically painful to the ears of those listening. Burns later commented on the play as a combination of "a number of themes explored in earlier work: the boy victim; the poignancy, bravery and senselessness of his sacrifice; state power" (1975, 67). We might add to this its role introducing multimedia collage to his work which previously, in novels like *Celebrations* (1967) and *Babel* (1969), had involved increasingly complex cut-up, fold-in and transcription practices using language. Published by John Calder, owner of Better Books where Nuttall performed his earliest People Shows, Burns' one-time break into theatre may even have been inspired by the People Shows he attended in previous years. The integration of these audiovisual techniques into Burns' writing might therefore be attributed to his cultural engagement on the periphery of the counterculture. While this peripheral status may have encouraged Burns on a formal level, however, the confidence it presumably gave him to engage with the Angry Brigade as subject matter was, for some in the counterculture, a step too far.

In an interview with David Madden in 1997, Burns recalled his choice of subject matter for *The Angry Brigade* in terms of a "natural sympathy for the group's aims, and even, though to a lesser extent, their methods. They were, inevitably, portrayed in the press as psychopaths and hoodlums. I wanted to correct this version of red-baiting by showing the true process of radicalisation" (1997a, 115). In spite of this desire to show the "true process", Burns never contacted any member of the Angry Brigade, preferring to pursue the kinds of aesthetic, political and emotional truths he had sought to uncover in his preceding works and using the same experimental techniques to unearth them. Unlike Burns' earlier novels, however, the techniques of collage and found material are not visible on the surface of the text. Instead, the novel appears in the form of an interview transcript—six voices: four men and two women—who describe their development from politically conscious dropouts to urban guerrilla fighters using convincingly informal language and reference points recognisable to anyone following the trial of the actual group. Burns also subtitled the work a "documentary novel" in reference to the many "documents" he collaged together in its creation. Such a cavalier approach to questions of documentary and literary truth did not serve to evoke the natural sympathies of Britain's far-left and anarchist writers, with figures like Tom Vague and Stuart Christie dismissing the work as an elaborate and malicious bourgeois lie.

On Burns' own terms, however, the work was his most "true" so far. As he described to David Madden, the use of tape recordings for greater accuracy and verisimilitude (a technique developed for *Palach*) allowed him a level of directness in his work he had been searching for throughout the previous decade:

> I resolved to write in a plain, accessible style, literally a 'conversational' style, via the tape recorder. The recorder was a godsend to me. I cut out the cut-up and found this other way of creating the 'ocean of raw material' I have always needed, so that I could 'find' the good stuff among the debris… I also discovered the wonderful music and subtlety of people's speech. (1997b, 134)

The novel's truth emerges from its closeness to life; a polyphony of recorded voices not emerging from the writer but from others around him. By bringing together these disparate voices, chopping them and changing them and fitting them into six recognisable characters, Burns is performing formally what many underground press writers were stating rhetorically; that "we are all the Angry Brigade now". The narrative of radicalisation is pieced together from the emotional and figurative resonances of everyday speech, often regarding everyday subjects too. As he did with Palach's self-immolation, Burns situated the terrorism of the Angry Brigade within a structure of feeling emanating from daily life, submerged within the surfaces of seemingly ordinary and stable contemporary living. The level of empathy inferred with the group was such that Burns' recordings mostly seem to be taken from his own groups of friends and colleagues. Rather than performing an anthropological infiltration of the working class, Burns draws some of his most potent material from seeming banalities:

> To give a rather curious example: I had a friend, a young woman, who had to visit the dentist on a number of occasions. This dismal experience was made worse by the fact that as she sat there the dentist and his nurse, between whom there seemed to be something cooking, would gossip away one to the other, excluding the patient. (Johnson 1981, 164)

This description of an awkward, uncomfortable and disempowering situation is transcribed into the novel as the voice of one of the women in the squat who is increasingly left out of conversations due to her lack of "commitment to the cause". From a patient stuck powerless in the dentist's chair to a conspirator cut out of vital information but too implicated to leave; the sense of "being aware there were things going on that she was not part of, being distressed and disturbed and a bit frightened" (Johnson 1981, 165) was transferred with only minor alterations. Burns' identification with the Angry Brigade as being "like us" is strikingly literal here. Not only are their voices "our own" but their experiences as terrorists exist in the same emotional landscape as our own lives.

Structurally, *The Angry Brigade* follows the standard terrorist morphology. An accumulating series of violent incidents build to a final grand failure. Its chapters are even arranged by titles indicating the process of escalation and acceleration: "Radicalize", "Organize", "Fraternize", "Mobilize", "Revolutionize", "Terrorize". From six radically-minded dropouts organising soup kitchens, drug counselling services and flyering, the group convinces itself of its moral rectitude and the desperation of the political situation. It then embarks upon increasingly destructive and eye-catching actions in pursuit of their revolutionary goal. The central tension between ideologically dogmatic Igor and working class activist Dave generates increasing one-upmanship, alienating the more liberal characters Mehta and Suzanne. A plan is developed wherein the group organise a protest march, incite it to violent confrontation and then use the resulting fracas as a distraction while they take the Permanent Secretary of the Ministry of Housing hostage and demand an improvement to housing conditions. The plan, initially successful, backfires when the group find the Permanent Secretary to be receptive to their demands and, short on ideas, the group then open the doors of the Town Hall and bring in demonstrators to form an ongoing occupation of the building. Once everything in the building is either smashed or covered in graffiti most of the occupiers leave, leaving the police free to raid the building. The Angry Brigade, barricaded in the basement, are eventually cornered and arrested. In court, the evidence is only sufficient to land David—the group's only genuinely working class member—in prison, where he remains for five years. Coming out, Dave finds that his former comrade Igor has turned the Angry Brigade into a genuinely violent, street-fighting terrorist group who machine-gun police and burn buses. It is at this point, confronted with what his former group has become, that Dave realises the effect that the group had on him:

> The lads could do it, but I wouldn't. For them it was a matter of believing in a myth because they wanted to believe in it. It was against my nature to die for the revolution, I would not die for the working class, I would live for it. It was this clash of beliefs that frightened me. I was convinced I would not shoot, and somehow they were convinced I would. (1973b, 183)

The turning away from violence at this last critical point restores the reader's faith in the humanity of Dave and the merit behind his original ideals. Arguably, the extreme pitch the terrorists' violence had to reach for the protagonist to have this realisation undermines the novel's realism and its didactic function. The line where violence becomes unacceptable is a point that a terrorist group would struggle to reach in reality. An open civil war between the Angry Brigade and the police fought across the streets of London was, historically, simply impossible.

Considering the aspirations of libertarian-left urban guerrilla groups and the minimal extent to which the actual Angry Brigade lived up to them, one might argue that this fantastical ending is both in keeping with hyperbolic Angry Brigade rhetoric and serves to eclipse the actual violence of their actions by contrast, lending them a certain sympathy or at least a plea for leniency.

The symbolic interaction between the novel's Angry Brigade and Burns' implied readership, an elite cultural milieu interested in literary experiment, can also be found in the variety of intertextual references on display including both Marcuse and the Situationists. Early in the novel a fictional Situationist even "came over from Paris and wanted us to change our line. They said we were far too confused, which we were" (1973b, 42). Reference to the Situationists is also made at the critical moment of the novel where the Permanent Secretary of the Ministry of Housing is held hostage. The group storm a boardroom where the Permanent Secretary is chairing a meeting and produce a fake hand grenade; "it was like the grenades issued to the British Army in Ireland. That was important, because it was based on the Situationist idea that you get hold of the resources of the State and use them against the State" (1973b, 96). The reference to avant garde artists at the moment of violence invites the potentially squeamish reader to consider the violence symbolically. That the hand grenade is fake also adds to the ludic qualities of the action, suggesting that the loaded quality of the gesture is, at its core, harmless and more in the nature of an elaborate joke than an actual terrorist threat. The fantasies which the Angry Brigade go on to indulge in after the success of this action equally convey a sense of playfulness and harmless unreality. The "fantastic leap of imagination, something that will make people jump right out of their skins," which the Angries search for is described in fantastic, cinematic images—"King Kong walking down Oxford Street, or a space ship landing on St Paul's" (1973b, 156)—which in the moment of their Situationist silliness, also demonstrates the cartoonish imaginations which lie behind the wild acts of terror. Informed by aesthetic theory but also pitifully immature, Burns allows his readership to identify with the Angry Brigade while also placing them at a safe, somewhat patronising distance.

As a final point of empathy between author and subject in *The Angry Brigade*, one can find a subtle metafictional reference to the author's technique appearing in the "Mobilize" chapter of the novel. A pamphlet on "The Violence of the State" which the group produces "to stop people thinking that all we were doing was sitting in our pads smoking dope," is handed out on the London underground in the form of "a Happening": "We'd tear a page in half, here's a half, here's a half, get together and read it" (1973b, 61). The character undertaking this experiment in political polemics, Dave, goes on to become the main character in the narrative. Using the same cut-up techniques that Burns used to construct the novel itself, the implication that the author and his terrorist protagonist are one and the same is unmistakable. Burns here implies that the writing of this novel is itself a radical and insurrectionary act. Nuttall's need to exorcise the terrorist figure as one engaged on work dangerously close to his own is mirrored here, although Burns seems less conflicted in his equation of writing and terror. It's here where we can address the second experimental novel in this chapter. Where Burns expresses this relationship in a coded manner, B.S. Johnson's novel, *Christie Malry's Own Double-Entry*, also published in 1973, uses the dynamic of literature-as-terror as its central theme. What Burns only alludes to, Johnson makes explicit.

Johnson's oeuvre represents an increasingly desperate pursuit of truth and authenticity in literature. From breaking out of the narrative in his second novel *Albert Angelo* to declaim "Fuck all this lying... telling stories is telling lies!" (2002, 167), to his novel *The Unfortunates* which was published unbound, Johnson's work is, in the words of Christie Malry himself, "a continuous dialogue with form" (2001, 166). The tragic farce, *Christie Malry...*, stands as the last completed novel Johnson produced and, fittingly, cuts to the bared heart of the novel's engagement with terrorism. The terrorist and the novelist both set out to change the world single handed, to force the world to conform with the image they have of it, yet neither can ever impose that image; they can only create an image, a violent image, and then submit its interpretation to a public that don't understand. For Johnson, fictionally imposing himself into his own text as an author-character, the struggle of the writer against the tradition of the novel form is a direct reflection of the terrorist struggling against the powers that be.

The novel centres around a "cell of one", the eponymous Christie Malry, "a simple person" (2001, 11) whose position as bookkeeper provides inspiration for a "Great Idea". Realising how he might settle his various scores with society, or "THEM", Christie opens an account between "THEM" and himself, debiting the injustices he suffers, which he translates into a monetary cost. In order to credit himself and balance the books, Christie must then inflict damage upon society commensurate with the value of injustice society has done him. Imposed between chapters throughout the novel are pages from Christie's bookkeeping activities so far. The first of these, for example, shows the "unpleasantness of general bank manager" (2001, 47) priced at £1, while Christie's refusal to pay the undertaker for his mother's funeral expenses credits him £1.71. Overall, however, society still owes Christie £8.67 after his first quarter. The farcical nature of the novel lies in this system's immediate descent into extremes. By Christie's fourth "Reckoning" of his accounts he has poisoned a London reservoir and caused the death of 20,479 innocent west Londoners, crediting £26,622.70 "calculated at the rate of £1.30 each being an allowance for the commercial value of the chemicals contained therein" (2001, 119). This massacre, however, comes nowhere near balancing the debit of £311,398 owed to Christie for the reason, "socialism not given a chance" (2001, 151). In the end, Christie's campaign of terror is cut short by a sudden bout of cancer, the author-character refuses to inform his readers whether or not the final bomb under Parliament goes off, and £352,392 is written off as bad debt. The simple yet potent metaphor of metaphysical accounting makes directly visible to the reader, to the penny, the processes of political and ethical valuation and re-evaluation undertaken by all terrorist protagonists in the acceleration of their conflict with the amorphous state (or "THEM"). Where other authors' success can be judged by their psychological realism, Johnson bypasses realism and instead presents these accounts as indisputable mathematical fact. This leaves the rest of the narrative with considerable room to expand beyond questions of terror and engage with existential and political self-interrogations. Johnson doesn't simply create a fictional terrorist, he has that terrorist question him about why he was created.

While throughout the novel Christie Malry takes pains to ridicule "the comic story of God" (2001, 29), Johnson is resolutely theological, or at least teleological, in his interrogation of how the subject can bring themselves to act in a chaotic universe. "We shall die untidily," Christie's mother tells him before her own (ironically very tidy) death, "when we do not properly expect it, in a mess, most things unresolved, unreckoned, reflecting that it is all chaos. Even if we understand that all is chaos, the understanding itself represents a denial of chaos, and must therefore be an illusion" (2001, 30). Christie's "Great Idea" gives us a numerical chart by which to measure his violent acts and personal experiences of oppression. Moral judgements are made for him. Like Pascal, who argues that the

Catholic Church does not exist to bring people closer to God but rather to do the work of believing for them, Christie's accounting book serves as a teleological supplement. It is a machine that converts discontent into violence without Christie even needing to think. Where Ian Purdie, reading Sorel in his prison cell, seeks to internalise and purify his revolutionary will, Christie simply does the maths. Thanks to his new moral certainty he can unashamedly take joy in his actions—"shall I experiment with explosive mice, thought Christie? Or other small rodents? Bomb-carrying blackbirds? The possibilities were endless" (2001, 123).[4] Christie's accounting is, from this perspective, an all-purpose substitute for commitment. Protagonist or antagonist, every other terrorist featured in this study is committed to a principle (whether they are true to that principle or not). The ironic inversion of accounting, the basic foundation of capitalism, as itself the basis for a terrorist's campaign of destruction, inverts the liberal tenet that finance is rational while principles are irrational. Christie reduces the world to pure economic self-interest in extremis, sacrificing innocent lives in pursuit of a balanced moral chequebook. Like Don Quixote, however, the reader is left in no doubt that we are on some level to appreciate Christie for this total commitment to a deranged idea, even as we are relieved to see his campaign of terror come to a close at the end of the narrative.

Johnson's disillusion with the political system after the passing of the Industrial Relations Bill is only one aspect of a wider spiral of failures and depression overtaking the author's life. Reading his correspondences and notebooks of the period reveals a deep anxiety about the potential for the country to slip into fascism and a conviction that MI5 were tapping his phone. It is at this point that he and Alan Burns begin to sit in on the proceedings of the Angry Brigade trial. An undated letter from Burns to Johnson which we can assume dates from this period shows the pair were also at this time reading urban guerrilla literature and handbooks:

> Thanks for the subversive lit. The manual of the urban guerrilla – the South American one – is very useful and the others come in handy – though I still don't know how to make a BOMB! I'm neck deep in every kinda crisis here, but there it is. It's a nice day. My bank has stopped my cheques. (1973a)

Looking through Johnson's own notes in preparation for the writing of *Christie Malry* we can see how this reading of terrorist literature was not undertaken as part of cursory background research, but engaged with on a personal level, its consequences thought through. Johnson was no stranger to this level of engagement; for his novel *Trawl* he spent three weeks on a trawler, suffering constant seasickness, in order that the trawler in his novel might be more than just metaphor and imagination. Here we see Johnson assessing himself as novelist, whether he is doing enough, and what a future career as an urban guerrilla would theoretically look like:

> The UG [urban guerrilla] must be careful not to appear strange and separated from ordinary life.
> The UG must live by his work or professional activity.
> The UG must be very searching and knowledgeable about the area in which he lives or operates.
> The UG should kill police chiefs and expropriate capitalist funds.
> Surprise compensates for the UG's inferiority to his enemy, who has no way to fight surprise.
> But the time is no longer to write novels; or to write at all? (Coe 2004, 317)

The listing form adopted here, with its staccato rhythm, economy of expression and repetitive usage of "UG", or urban guerrilla, suggest that Johnson is inspired here by the writings of Carlos Marighella.[5] Marighella's *Mini-Manual of the Urban Guerrilla* (1969) was one of a number of works circulated among the terrorist underground and, as has been described earlier, was idolised and imitated by European left-wing militants. Considering *Christie Malry*'s existential overtones, Marighella's own theory of the guerrilla is suitably vitalist, suggesting that "it is better to err acting than to do nothing for fear of erring," for "without initiative there is no guerrilla warfare" (2002, 70). Powerful words for a disheartened activist to read. If "all life is chaos", as the novel so often restates, then every action is an erring action based on an illusion. The act's potency, however, is derived from its very ability to exist within an illusory universe; the act is the only true remedy for doubt.

The existential dilemmas which the terrorist figure inhabits in Johnson's novel are directly connected to the role of the writer in the world. Johnson imposes himself into the novel as a seemingly omnipotent figure, only to be argued with by his protagonist and ushered out of Christie's deathbed scene by a worried nurse. She didn't understand, we are told, "that he could not die without me" (2001, 180). By his own assessment, Johnson's commitment to formal innovation is promethean in scope, workmanlike in practice and historically necessary. And yet, in Johnson's own novels it is this hyperbole which is the butt of every joke. He makes his own hubris funny, but nevertheless continues to hold the same opinions. The same self-criticism, more serious in tone, is visible in his memoirs:

> The novelist cannot legitimately or successfully embody present-day reality in exhausted forms. If he is serious, he will be making a statement which attempts to change society towards a condition he conceives to be better, and he will be making at least implicitly a statement of faith in the evolution of the form in which he is working. (1973, 16)

The novelist's commitment to formal innovation is unavoidable if one is to take one's task seriously. It is also implicitly tied to a political function which allies innovation and progressive change, and by contrast, appears ridiculous to traditionalist and conservative viewpoints. The ability for any of this fiction-work to actually have an impact or influence in the way it has been theorised is ultimately unknowable; an article of faith. Whether a writer engages with these responsibilities or not, the act of writing itself carries them implicitly. One is forced to take a position, consciously or not, as to the values one embodies in one's work. The commitment to literature as a political catalyst is itself Quixotic, an act which no rational accounting could call realistic. Yet, one is bound to act, to err acting. Taking *Christie Malry* as an "implicit... statement of faith" in the political potency of writing, an act as irrational as any urban guerrilla taking up arms against a sea of troubles, some of the lasting appeal of the terrorist in literature becomes visible. The particular historical circumstances by which the 1970s in Britain encouraged the use of the terrorist as a symbol are a vital component in the analysis of this trend, but it is in the moments when the writer identifies with the terrorist not only in their cause but in their hopelessness that the full poetry of the form is realised.

Notes

1. Although no novels expressly focus on international left-wing terrorists as a threat to Britain, they do occasionally appear as bit-part players. In Jack Davies' *Esther, Ruth and Jennifer* (1979), for example, two members

of the Japanese Red Army, disguised "with thick glasses and buck teeth" (1979, 47), aid an American gangster in hijacking a North Sea oil rig.
2. Also held in the Rylands archive is Jeff Nuttall's "Project sTigma". The project seemingly consisted of a book in which anyone could write their name and become a member after paying £1 and swearing "I undertake to go through the sTigma at my own risk to life, sanity and clothing". The handwriting of many of the signatures suggests the book may have been brought out most often after a few drinks at a party. The signatures include a "J. Prescott", perhaps belonging to Angry Brigade member Jake Prescott. Also included, however, are signatures for "Mick Jagger" and "Keith Richard" [sic] which do not appear genuine.
3. The Act's excessively punitive fines and open-ended wording, which were the focus of the campaign against it, rendered the new legislation unworkable in practice and it was repealed by the Labour government in 1974. Johnson, who committed suicide in 1973, would not live to see himself proven right.
4. Chris Morris' 2010 comedy about hapless terrorists, *Four Lions*, features a bomb-carrying blackbird, perhaps as in homage to *Christie Malry*. His co-writer, David Quantick, is a noted B.S. Johnson fan and has contributed essays to *BSJ: The B.S. Johnson Journal*.
5. Darlington (2014) suggests Che Guevara's *Guerrilla Warfare* may be the text referred to, being the most successful overground text. Subsequent research into underground terrorist literature, however, has convinced me that Marighella's *Mini-Manual* is the text most likely being referred to.

Bibliography

Anon. 1971a. Angry Politics. *IT/111*. September 9.
Anon. 1971b. One Big Frame Up: The Prison Letters of Jake Prescott and Ian Purdie. *Oz 37*. September.
Ansorge, Peter. 1975. *Disrupting the Spectacle: Five Years of Experimental and Fringe Theatre in Britain*. London: Pitman.
Burns, Alan. 1973a. Letter to B.S. Johnson. Held in British Library.
———. 1973b. *The Angry Brigade*. London: Calder and Boyars.
———. 1975. Essay. In *Beyond the Words*, ed. Giles Gordon. London: Hutchinson.
Burns, Alan, and Charles Sugnet (eds.). 1981. *The Imagination on Trial*. London: Allison and Busby.
Carr, Gordon. 2010. *The Angry Brigade: A History of Britain's First Urban Guerrilla Group*. Oakland: PM Press.
Carter, Angela. 1982. *The Infernal Desire Machines of Doctor Hoffman*. London: Penguin.

Clutterbuck, Richard. 1973. *Protest and the Urban Guerrilla*. New York: Abelard-Schuman.
Coe, Jonathan. 2004. *Like a Fiery Elephant: The Story of B.S. Johnson*. London: Picador.
Darlington, Joseph. 2014. Cell of One: B.S. Johnson, Christie Malry and the Angry Brigade. In *B.S. Johnson and Post-war Literature: Possibilities of the Avant Garde*, ed. Julia Jordan and Martin Ryle. London: Palgrave Macmillan.
Davies, Jack. 1979. *Esther, Ruth and Jennifer*. London: W.H. Allen.
Dickinson, Robert. 1997. *Imprinting the Sticks: The Alternative Press Beyond London*. Aldershot: Arena.
During, Simon. 2007. Socialist Ends: The British New Left, Cultural Studies and the Emergence of Academic Theory. *Postcolonial Studies* 10 (1): 23–39.
Fairlight, Harry. 1975. Letter to Jeff Nuttall. Held in John Rylands Library. March 11.
Hanson, Steve. 2013. *Jeff Nuttall and the Yorkshire Counterculture*. Bradford: Nowt Press.
Houen, Alex. 2001. *Terrorism and Modern Literature*. Oxford: Oxford University Press.
Johnson, B.S. 1973. *Aren't You Rather Young to Be Writing Your Memoirs?* London: Hutchinson.
———. 1981. Interview with Alan Burns. In *The Imagination on Trial*, ed. Alan Burns and Charles Sugnet. London: Allison and Busby.
———. 2001. *Christie Malry's Own Double-Entry*. London: Picador.
———. 2002. *Albert Angelo. Omnibus*. London: Picador.
Kurstow, Mike. 1967. Letter to Jeff Nuttall. Held in John Rylands Library. November 9.
Laing, R.D. 1981. *The Politics of Experience and the Bird of Paradise*. London: Penguin.
Lee, C.P. 2002. *Shake Rattle and Rain*. London: Harding Simpole.
Mack, Andrew. 1974. The Non-strategy of Urban Guerrilla Warfare. In *Urban Guerrilla: Studies on the Theory, Strategy and Practice of Political Violence in Modern Societies*, ed. Johan Niezing. Rotterdam: Rotterdam University Press.
Madden, David W. 1997a. Alan Burns: An Introduction. *The Review of Contemporary Literature* 17 (2): 108–121.
———. 1997b. An Interview with Alan Burns. *The Review of Contemporary Literature* 17 (2): 122–145.
Marighella, Carlos. 2002. *Mini-Manual of the Urban Guerrilla*. Montreal: Abraham Guillen and Arm the Spirit Press.
Mole. 1970. *Mole Express*, No. 12. April.
Mole. 1971. *Mole Express*, No. 27. December.
Mottram, Eric. 1975. Letter to Jeff Nuttall. Held in John Rylands Library. April 29.

Nuttall, Jeff. 1968. *Bomb Culture*. London: Paladin.
———. 1975a. Letter to Harry Fairlight. Held in John Rylands Library.
———. 1975b. *Man, Not Man*. Llanfynydd: Unicorn.
———. 1975c. *Snipe's Spinster*. London: Calder and Boyars.
———. 1979. *Performance Art, Volume 2: Scripts*. London: John Calder.
———. n.d. *Project sTigma* notebook. Held in John Rylands Library.
Palmer, Tony. 1971. *The Trials of Oz*. London: Blond and Briggs.
Preece, Julian. 2012. *Baader-Meinhof and the Novel*. London: Palgrave Macmillan.
Purdie, Ian. 1971. Prison Letters. *IT/111*. September 9.
Roszak, Theodore. 1970. *The Making of a Counter Culture*. London: Faber and Faber.
Rubin, Jerry. 1970. *Do It!: Scenarios of the Revolution*. New York: Simon and Schuster.
Schiele, Jinnie. 2005. *Off-Centre Stages: Fringe Theatre at the Open Space and the Roundhouse, 1968–1983*. Hatfield: University of Hertfordshire Press.
Spates, James L. 1976. Counterculture and Dominant Culture Values: A Cross-National Analysis of the Underground Press and Dominant Culture Magazines. *American Sociological Review* 41: 868–883.
Taber, Robert. 1970. *The War of the Flea: Guerrilla Warfare Theory and Practice*. London: Paladin.
Trocchi, Alexander. n.d. Project Sigma Membership List. Held in John Rylands Library.
———. 1991. Sigma: A Tactical Blueprint. In *Invisible Insurrection of a Million Minds: A Trocchi Reader*, ed. Andrew Murray Scott, 177–191. Edinburgh: Polygon.
Wilbur, Seymore. 1972. The £1,000,000 Lie. *IT/144*.

CHAPTER 6

Environmentalists and Conservationists: Terrorising the Countryside

> And that will be England gone,
> The shadows, the meadows, the lanes,
> The guildhalls, the carved choirs.
> There'll be books; it will linger on
> In galleries; but all that remains
> For us will be concrete and tires.
> (Larkin 1972)

So ends the poem commissioned by the HMSO to open their report, "How do You Want to Live?". The report focuses on the ever-diminishing amount of green space in British towns and Larkin's mournful poetry no doubt intended to convey this loss. An unexpurgated version of the poem, newly entitled "Going, Going", would appear two years later in his collection *High Windows*. A comparison of the two versions reveals that, before publication, the editors of the original government document saw fit to remove the fatalistic final stanza where we are told that "greeds and garbage are too thick-strewn to be swept up now" (1974). They also remove Larkin's references to "spectacled grins" and "grey area grants" (1974) which perhaps cut too close to the bone. In Larkin scholarship these edits have come to represent the poet's clear-eyed conservationist pessimism falling afoul of a squeamish government loath to face the real threat of environmental collapse. Larkin's work can be seen as a lone voice in the wilderness. Wherever the truth lies with the editing of this particular document, however, the notion that Larkin's apocalyptic imagination was somehow out of place in the 1970s is a considerable mischaracterisation. If anything, it is in the 1970s when apocalyptic environmentalism goes mainstream.

By 1974, when "Going, Going" would first appear in full, environment-oriented public debate was dominated by the dystopian mode. The message that permanent growth was impossible on a planet with finite resources lay at the centre of ecological thinking. It even appeared within the very HMSO report Larkin's poem was supposedly too pessimistic for. At the same moment, the post-war baby boom was becoming visible in demographic statistics. Reports of exponential population growth began to stoke the same fears which motivated Malthus a hundred and seventy years earlier.

In Britain, environmentalism had previously been only one aspect of a larger set of conservationist concerns. The changes are visible in the constitution of groups founded between 1945 and 1969 on the one hand, and those appearing after 1970 on the other. As well as long-standing conservationist bodies The National Trust, RSPCA and the RSPB, 1957 saw the Civic Trust founded to conserve and improve buildings and spaces within the urban environment, the British Trust for Conservation Volunteers appeared in 1959 for the upkeep of green spaces and, in 1966, the Conservation Society formed to campaign on political issues of conservation and environment. Each of these groups held ecological convictions, although these were undoubtedly secondary to larger conservation and national heritage concerns. The 1970s, however, sees Britain forming its first Friends of the Earth group in 1971, the Green Party (then called the Ecology Party) in 1973, a UK-based branch of Greenpeace in 1977, and the Green Alliance think-tank in 1978. Each of these new groups come very definitely under a radical mantle of environmentalism as opposed to the, by contrast, largely conservative heritage and conservationist movements of earlier years. The "greater emphasis on popular activism" (1998, 16) attributed to these groups by Peter Rawcliffe is largely due to the apocalyptic vision emerging in mainstream ecological thinking. Two very different images of the future inspired the groups. The timescale of the heritage movements' historical imagination spread far beyond the horizon, conserving buildings and landscapes for generations to come. By contrast, the environmentalist movement saw a world already verging on cataclysm; many reports predicted a mass extinction event coming before the millennium.

The process of polemical radicalisation visible in new environmentalist groups corresponds with those trends we've already witnessed across other spheres in the 1970s.

Ecological catastrophes were everywhere in British science fiction. In *Solar Flares*, Andrew Butler describes how "the environment itself [often] becomes a character in the narrative, especially as an antagonist to the hero" (2012, 120). Michael Moorcock's series of Jerry Cornelius books depict a large variety of futures for Britain, all of which involve ecological apocalypse. The end of civilisation sometimes results from social breakdown, sometimes scientific mistake, occasionally through the exhaustion of fossil fuel reserves: regardless of how it happens, the destruction always turns the environment against us. *The English Assassin* (1972) and *The Condition of Muzak* (1977), his 1970s contributions to the series, also feature his time-travelling anarcho-terrorist heroine Una Persson. Her spin-off novel, *The Adventures of Una Persson and Catherine Cornelius in the Twentieth Century* (1976), places the collapse of civilisation in an anarchist context. "Civilisation is destroyed and most of those who would destroy it are now gone themselves. Their disciples scarcely know why they are fighting... I feared anarchy, but apathy is much worse" (1976, 193). Nature itself, Moorcock implies, is tending towards catastrophe. Anarchist terrorism is simply a reflection of entropic forces already in motion and, for Una Persson, the continuation of struggle—"anarchy"—is all that remains other than the "apathy" of sinking back into non-existence.

Terrorists appear in British sci-fi calamity fiction less than one might presume. Other than Moorcock's fun-loving revolutionaries the closest one gets to a terrorist is Davis and Pedlar's saboteur in *The Dynostar Menace* (1975). Set in the 1990s, Earth has exhausted its fossil fuels and is staking everything on the Dynostar experiment: a fusion power station housed on an orbital satellite. A week from Dynostar's launch, the environmentalist "Council of Twelve" (1975, 22) reports that its energy beam, if fired, will destroy the ozone layer. Rather than concede to the demands of environmentalists one scientist goes rogue, sabotaging the station and murdering his fellow scientists in order to keep Project Dynostar on track. Again, as with Una Persson, David and Pedlar present natural forces inevitably tending towards society's end; the difference with their terrorist lies in his commitment to speeding that process up through science. By the end of the novel the terrorist might have been brought to justice but, with the failure of Dynostar, the human race is nevertheless doomed to return to the dark ages.

The environmental collapse of civilisation wasn't only a matter of concern within science fiction however. The politics of small-scale societies and cooperative organisation which the ecology movement celebrated intersected with New Left sentiments (a crossover made clear in underground press periodicals such as *Gandalf's Garden* which married psychic liberation and horticulture). The sense of a Britain in decline, symbolised in polluted and desolate landscapes, also evoked a certain post-colonial malaise. The Oil Crisis of 1973 which drove oil prices up 500% (Ikenberry 1986, 105) took on special resonance for ecologists. As Hannah Gay points out, the crisis of 1973 is foregrounded in the green imagination by the dramatic crash of the oil tanker *Torrey Canyon* in 1967. "There was a major environmental disaster along the Cornish coast caused by [this] major oil spill" which, for many commentators, was readily attributable to the "one notable British resource being exploited in this period; ...North Sea oil and gas" (2012, 98). Other ideological outlooks have been seen to connect distinct events from the late 1960s and early 1970s in order to attribute some overall meaning to the sudden failure of the post-war consensus; for the environmental movement these developments were directly scored into the landscape. Not only is the identity of Britain at threat, but the very land itself and the creatures that walk upon it are all dying and becoming toxic. The imperative to act is immediate, and the scale of action required is revolutionary.

The terrorist who takes up arms against the forces of industrialism on behalf of the natural environment is reacting to a truly existential threat. As we shall see, this threat is represented by wildly different political forces across the range of 1970s eco-terrorist literature, yet the threat itself remains consistent: it is the threat of modernity. The modern world appears as an occupying force upon the land; a merciless destroyer of nature on both a figurative and a literal level. This extreme view is not only visible within activist circles, but appears throughout the scientific literature. 1970s ecology, to the contemporary reader, is striking in its conscious use of apocalyptic imagery. Reinforced by a mutual confirmation of increasingly apocalyptic predictions and driven by an urgency of purpose, writers of ecological studies in the 1970s share many traits with the propagandists of other political causes. The writing itself generates terror and this terror seeks to attain a radical political goal.

One of the founding texts of the environmentalist movement was Rachel Carson's *Silent Spring* (1962); a study which set the tone for the new radicalism. Carson's main target of the book, industrial pesticides and herbicides, are described as "a new kind of havoc" (1965, 87). The book moves from chapter to chapter demonstrating the accumulating effects these biocides have first on the target area, then upon the food chain through the effects of bioaccumulation, then upon the wider environment through carcinogens, and then, finally, the widespread damage these pesticides might inflict upon a number of species, including humans. Chapter by chapter the stakes grow higher until, by the end of the book, the "silent spring" of the future has become visible with a land poisoned and stripped of its living creatures. Interestingly, this accumulative effect of the chapters relies upon the same narrative momentum as many terrorist novels. Here, however, the technique serves not only as an effective means of plot development but also encourages an ecologically-minded awareness of consequences within complex systems. It effectively narrativises systems thinking. Hannah Gay, who describes *Silent Spring* as "one of the most important science books of the twentieth century" (2012, 108), suggests that the dynamism of 1970s ecology movements may be traced back to the method of communication derived from this book. Carson encouraged readers to think of the natural world as a complex series of interconnected networks, all impacting upon each other in unexpected ways. Arguably, her popular success lay in the fact that she concentrated upon the interconnectedness of destruction. The destruction was inaccurate but the systems weren't.

The use of newly developing ecological science to predict global environmental collapse reached its peak in 1972. Two influential texts, *The Limits to Growth* and *A Blueprint for Survival*, are particularly notable for their apocalyptic vision. Funded by Volkswagen and commissioned by The Club of Rome (the same Club of Rome denigrated in *The Dynostar Menace* as they "didn't know what the hell they were talking about back then" (1975, 22)), *Limits to Growth* foregrounded the "exponential" nature of twentieth-century population growth and economic expansion. It concluded with a dire warning of what should happen were it to continue unheeded:

> Accepting the nature-imposed limits to growth requires no more effort than letting things take their course and waiting to see what will happen. The most probable result of that decision, as we have tried to show here, will be an uncontrollable decrease in population and capital. (Meadows et al. 1972, 169)

These predictions arguably stem from two factors working in harmony; the relatively undeveloped methodologies of new ecological science being pushed to their limits, and the socially-derived willingness to accept and pursue radical conclusions. Methodologically, both *Limits to Growth* and *Blueprint for Survival*—a text predicting "a succession of famines, epidemics, social crises and wars" (1972, 15)—make great use of statistics, all of which appear to predict exponential growth. These dramatic predictions are explained through the relatively new concept of "feedback loops" which would seemingly allow such unprecedented expansion to occur. The choice to believe these models and then publish them alongside visions of environmental cataclysm, however, is undoubtedly a reflection of larger social anxieties. The deep political and social divisions of the 1970s encourage exaggeration where, in more stable times, cooler heads may have prevailed. Politically, this exaggeration is visible on both right and left—it lies at the heart of the terror novel—so it is in a way unsurprising to see it appear within environmentalist texts also.

Conceptually, apocalyptic environmental writing inverts the tradition of the natural sublime. Where, for the likes of Wordsworth, nature itself is the source of sublime excess—equal parts awe and terror—the desolated landscapes first foreseen in *Silent Spring* are testimony to a more awesome and terrifying power: that of mass industrialisation. Larkin's endless remains of concrete and tires sit Ozymandias-like amidst the desert that once was England. Aspects of everyday living from motorways and factories to even other people are imbued with terrifying properties. When not grouped into the sublimely expanding mass of "population", people are often referred to as "consumers". This metonym, utilised rhetorically, transmogrifies humans into beasts whose sole function is to unknowingly consume the whole earth. Edmund Burke describes a similar process in his *Philosophical Enquiry*, pointing to sublime terror as a form of possession: "no passion so effectively robs the mind of all its powers of acting and reasoning as fear" (2008, 53). Fear and disgust are the natural responses to the terrifying, according to Burke, and notably these can emerge as easily from thoughts as they can from physical pain and threat:

> The only difference between pain and terror, is, that things which cause pain operate on the mind, by the intervention of the body; whereas things that cause terror generally affect he bodily organs by the operation of the

mind suggesting the danger; but both agreeing, either primarily, or secondarily, in producing a tension, contraction, or violent emotion of the nerves, they agree likewise in everything else. (2008, 120)

The fear of impending natural disaster, reinforced by scientific projections, manifests as palpably as actual physical desolation in the 1970s radical-ecological imagination. As a result, radical reaction to such circumstances should be expected as surely as one would flinch from physical pain.

One novel stands as a testimony to radical environmentalist resistance over all others, Edward Abbey's *The Monkey Wrench Gang* (1975). Unlike the rest of the books in our study, Abbey's is wholeheartedly American. It is drawn on here to stand in for the hollow centre of British eco-terrorist writing from this period. In spite of producing large numbers of texts with environmentalist themes—some, as we'll see, featuring terrorists—Britain produces no quintessential eco-terrorist thriller during this period. Abbey's book, widely read and discussed in the UK, can be seen to play this role.

Popular with both British and American audiences on its first publication in 1975, it later went on to inspire the Earth First! movement—Abbey personally contributing to their journal—and directly influenced the 1990s eco-terrorist group, the Earth Liberation Front. ELF even referred to their sabotage actions as "monkeywrenching" in homage to the novel (List 1993, 149).[1] Drawing on the dual American mythologies of Thoreau's *Walden* and Wild West cowboys, Abbey's novel follows a rag-tag group of environmental terrorists from early acts of vandalism through to a failed demolition of a bridge, a final dramatic chase scene and a shootout with the FBI. The protagonists, a Mormon outdoorsman, a Vietnam veteran, an idealistic medical doctor and his hippy partner, first come together on a rafting trip in the Arizona desert where a mutual desire to demolish a newly-built hydroelectric dam launches them on their campaign. Figuratively, the characters stand in for aspects of 1970s American life sidelined by growing state-corporate power structures and the wilderness in which they conduct their campaign of sabotage comes to stand for America itself. The combination of these somewhat clichéd symbolic underpinnings and the novel's narrative structure alleviate some of the weaknesses of the writing itself. Each chapter revolves around a new act of industrial sabotage, increasing in scale, following the standard terrorist morphology. As such, the reader is encouraged to continue with the text through the promise of bigger and better acts of destruction to come. In searching for an ideological underpinning to the novel, however, there seems only to be a general misanthropy communicated through images of environmental desolation both real and imagined. In Abbey's America, everyone is implicated in the pollution of the land, including the Native Americans:

> He hadn't remembered so many power lines. They stride across the horizon in multicolumn grandeur, looped together by the swoop and gleam of high-voltage cables charged with energy from the Glen Canyon Dam, from the Navajo Power Plant, from the Four Corners and Shiprock plants, bound south and westwards from the burgeoning Southwest and California. The blazing cities feed on the defenceless interior.... The real trouble with the goddamned Indians, reflected Hayduke, is that they are no better than the rest of us. The real trouble is that the Indians are just as stupid and greedy and cowardly and dull as us white folks. (1975, 21)

The impact of industrialisation in terms of pollutants and deforestation is conflated in Abbey's novel with human habitation in general which, strewn across the American landscape, is a metaphorical desecration of the libertarian values which that landscape represents. In spite of its environmentalist sentiments, the overarching message of *The Monkey Wrench Gang* is the same as any number of John Wayne or Clint Eastwood films. When America's in danger it is up to the hard man with the gun to set things straight.

This returns us to the question of why the U.K. produced no serious thriller to match Abbey's terrorist imagination. Dystopian imagery certainly abounds in British literature of the 1970s, but in terms of terror novels which react to environmental politics the trend is against Abbey's thriller mode. Firstly, they are consistently written in the comic mode and, secondly, the majority are conservative in outlook. This chapter will look at three of these: Maureen Duffy's *I Want to Go to Moscow* (1973), Tom Sharpe's *Blott on the Landscape* (1975) and Emma Tennant's *The Last of the Country House Murders* (1974). Just as questions of environmental destruction evoked in Edward Abbey a particularly American response, each of these novels embody conceptions of England from across the political spectrum. If terror novels implicitly invite questions of what a nation is, the environmentally-conscious terror novel extends this question to the land itself. When England's green and pleasant land is under threat, which will be forsaken first; the greenness or the pleasantries?

A NATION OF ANIMAL LOVERS

The first of these novels, *I Want to Go to Moscow*, is the seventh of Maureen Duffy's experimental oeuvre. An urban writer, Duffy's previous novels trace the lives of men and women negotiating metropolitan modernity. The sudden shift into terror-themed environmentalist comedy is not necessarily out of keeping with her previous works, however. As will be seen, the London counterculture was growing increasingly eco-conscious in the early 1970s, and this wasn't purely driven by idealism either. Dennis Rodwell writes about how the city in which Duffy was born, raised, worked and wrote underwent dramatic change at this time:

> London developed increasingly throughout the 1960s and '70s as a monocentric metropolitan city, one in which the key functions are separated – especially work and residence – and where the physical heart, the City, only functions on weekdays and small-scale artisan businesses have been driven out. (2010, 13)

The community-centric working class London of Duffy's childhood, nostalgically depicted in her first novel *That's How It Was* (1962), was being pushed further and further out from an increasingly commercial centre. Simultaneously, civic architecture's love affair with Brutalism was leading to the widespread destruction of Victorian era housing, widely dismissed as slums, in favour of the concrete uniformity of high-rise estates (Marwick 1998, 449). Central planning encouraged as much destruction of the urban environment as the rural, all in the name of progress. Looking back at the period in her memoirs, Doris Lessing describes how "up and down this happy land, people whose hearts beat day and night with love and concern for the working classes were saying, 'We'll clear them all out, we'll clean it all up'" (1998, 358). Urban dwellers were perhaps for the first time finding themselves in natural political alliance with the inhabitants of the countryside in their struggle against land clearances and mass compulsory purchase orders.

Concerns for the natural world were echoed in the London counterculture of the late 1960s, as depicted in Duffy's second novel *The Single Eye* (1964). Love and flowers bloomed in pop culture iconography.

The Kink's *Village Green Preservation Society* (1968) was an attempt to connect the burgeoning, largely metropolitan hippy culture with conservationist movements of a more traditional, small town England type. Even Doctor Who began to convey an environmentalist message; "in 'The Dalek's Master Plan' from 1966 the Doctor warns his companions not to go outside when [they] land in 1960s urban England because 'the whole atmosphere is entirely poisonous'" (Jorgenson 2012, 13). The popular culture of the U.K. in the early years of the 1970s was everywhere reinforcing the environmental concerns brought to light through campaigning literature. Although, unlike *Limits to Growth* or *Blueprint for Survival*, these messages were usually delivered in a more friendly, optimistic and, in many ways, more "English" manner. The epic scenery of the Wild West which American campaigners like Edward Abbey sought to defend was in Britain replaced with country gardens, Tolkeinesque shires and the pastoral scenes of Merrie England.

The direct action campaigns undertaken by environmentalist groups in the early 1970s which provided Duffy with her literary inspiration were equally committed to a media-friendly mode of resistance. The first of the actions, which also spurred the creation of Friends of the Earth, was led by Graham Searle in 1971. It started at a public seminar held at the Institute of Contemporary Arts. Discussing Cadbury Schweppes' recent decision not to recycle its fizzy drinks bottles:

> [Searle stood up] and said: 'Well, I'm going to take my bottle Saturday morning over to Cadbury Schweppes' [factory].' We got 50 yards of bottles quite closely set, it looked like a phenomenal sea of bottles. It made a terrific photograph. It went straight into the papers and that was that. People started ringing us up in the hundreds. (Rawcliffe 1998, 5)

Spurred on by this "happening", various groups began to use the non-violent methods now known as "guerrilla gardening". In *Radical Gardening* George McKay describes a number of these groups, including:

> A small group in 1972–1973 in London who dressed in green boiler suits like urban Robin Hoods and called themselves the Street Farmers... inspired by the Situationists and *les événements* of Paris 1968. Their ideas seem to have included ploughing up urban streets and planting instead fruit trees and vegetables. (2011, 122)

Planting also took on a radical role in the defence of squatted buildings. A thoroughly established and well-kept vegetable garden, it was argued, legally represented a visible signifier of the current inhabitants' non-transient status. Gardening became a way to fight for squatter's rights. Indeed, by the publication of *I Want to Go to Moscow* in 1973, the links between radical environmentalism, the counterculture, English pastoralism and traditional conservation were as visible among the packed terraced housing of London as they were in Hardyesque rural villages of the South West or the strip-mined and polluted industrial North.

In *I Want to Go to Moscow*, Duffy weaves these different bodies of resistance together into a single terror cell named All Heaven in a Rage.[2] The protagonist, Chuff, spends the first quarter of the novel in prison for his role as driver in a series of mob-related crimes. Set against the corruption of the prison staff and the violence of the other inmates, Chuff's desire to "keep his head down and keep his nose clean" (1978) soon establishes him as the archetypical hard-man with a heart of gold. Hearing of his criminal proficiency and reputation for non-violence, AHIAR (as they are abbreviated) conduct a daring jailbreak involving a turncoat prison vicar and a helicopter. Flown in secret to a large country house somewhere in southern England, Chuff is then enlisted in AHIAR, helping them to conduct their operations. At first, Chuff agrees to help only in return for his own safety and the promise of later cash payment. However, as he soon becomes romantically involved with fellow terrorist Philomela, he soon starts to become radicalised himself. Each successful mission brings him a deeper understanding of animal rights and leads him to fall further in love. The rhythms of pacing, tension and overall accumulation of action are consistent with the standard terrorist narrative morphology, the only difference being Duffy's unusual cast of terrorist characters.

The characters of Duffy's novel embody the same rural/urban that radical conservationism was seen to involve in the early 1970s. The result is a cast reminiscent of an Agatha Christie novel or music hall farce. Chuff begins as a representative of the working class, but also stands in for the uninitiated reader not yet familiar with AHIAR and their animal-rights politics. Philomela, young, sassy and a committed member of the "free love" generation, takes on the role of ideological expositor while providing some mild titillation between actions. The rest of the cast include the genial pamphleteer Reverend Raphael, the bellicose tactician Major Cracknell, and the impish dowagers Miss Cracknell and

Princess Halflinger by whom the organisation is funded. Duffy even employs the neighbourly bobby-on-the-beat archetype as occasional antagonist, all keeping with the farcical setting and tone. As a result, the Major's "calculated escalation" (1978, 57) of property destruction takes on the character of a parlour game with each action needing to grow exponentially; from the releasing of animals at a local factory farm to the airborne pamphleting of all London to the final plan to burn down the Ministry for Agriculture. The slightly dotty officer class invent increasingly elaborate plans which the grumbling Chuff and Philomela then have to put into action.

Behind the comedic framework of the text, however, Duffy also engages with distinct traditions of both English and international radicalism. Indeed, the seemingly innocuous Englishry of the text disguises a number of symbolic inversions. The reference to visionary and radical William Blake is but one of a patchwork of intertexts. Chuff reads Kafka's *The Trial* in his prison cell, Purcell's libretto to Dido's Lament is sung at the novel's close; there is a sense of English heritage communicated through these references which draws together the traditional cultural institutions of Britain and adds to them the radical tradition is which is usually excluded from heritage narratives. The printing press upon which their communiqués and pamphlets are produced bears living testimony to the traces of this literary underground, a society beneath the official history:

> It's an old one that's been used for years by different underground organisations. It printed IRA material in the twenties and leaflets for the Jarrow march. Then it was used for Spanish republican news sheets. During the war the Free French had it. When the war ended Spies for Peace took it over for a while until it passed to Grow Up and Love groups. It'll drop out of sight until someone needs it. So it can't ever be traced to the printer. (1978, 149)

There is a clear process of inclusion and exclusion occurring here (the inclusion of the IRA "in the twenties" is a snub to the IRA of the seventies, for example) yet the scope of the list is broad enough to suggest a general anti-establishment tradition. The printing press metonymically reproduces British radical history. The call to burn down the Ministry is met with the cry, "Oh Gawd... Guy Fawkes again" (1978, 169). The violence of the AHIAR group, targeting property only (a common trait of sympathetic terrorists in 1970s fiction), is submerged in a history of resistance. The association of the country house with tradition is also engaged here. As a terrorist novel, *I Want to Go to Moscow* sidesteps questions about the morality of violence intermeshing both alternative and official histories. Its use of historical reference points suggest that, like it or not, political violence is a part of British history too.

The novel's relationship to violence is framed so as not to evoke moral discomfort. Chuff may be uncertain about his commitment to environmentalism and animal rights, but he retains an unshakable belief in the sanctity of human life. The roots of his conscientious objection are institutional, starting in the military: "there's nothing clever about violence. Any mug can be trained to kill, I saw that in the army" (1978, 99) and developing further in prison life.[3] It is this double incarceration—military and penal—which symbolically connects Chuff to the animals he rescues. During the initial mass release of mink from a fur farm Chuff describes how the "hundreds of [animal] feet drummed softly... as they ran up and down their cells" and recalled the "fits of banging that overtook the nick at moments of communal despair" (1978, 83). The brute animal reactions of fear and pain evoke Chuff's empathy. He too, he feels, has been trapped in a cage. It is this identification which helps to convey the more abstract environmentalist messages of the text on an emotional level; using the animal in pain as a symbolic victim on whose part the terrorist group is acting. Wider themes of intransigent power structures and social oppression are subsumed into this cause on a thematic level. The Major is careful to mention that "peaceful social pressure over many years has failed" (1978, 53) before outlining his plans, sounding suspiciously like a member of the Angry Brigade. The impossibility of a democratic process of compromise is taken for granted and rapidly passed over. The perception of oppressive state power and even totalitarianism finds fulfilment in the symbolism of the trapped animal.

By foregrounding animal rights over more abstract environmental causes, *I Want to Go to Moscow*'s political message is more didactic than contemplative. For a terrorist novel to be unashamedly championing the cause of its protagonists is unusual. It shifts the usual balance of sympathetic characters and unsympathetic action which many of the other, more tonally serious novels depend on for their drama. Edward Abbey, for example, refuses to condone the actions undertaken by his terrorist protagonists while making his broader ideological sympathies clear. Abbey's loving descriptions of the Western landscape and his disgust at the modern industrialised world contrast with his characters' inexcusable acts. Duffy's novel, on the other hand, relies upon its characters as positive examples and thing the characters say they believe are supposed to be taken as valid political positions. As a result, the narrative amalgamates too many disparate interests to maintain a cohesive critique. The terrorist cell is a mix of all classes and all political outlooks, standing against modernity and tradition simultaneously. Where other novels could pass this off as characterisation, Duffy is earnest in the way she shares her character's views. Charming and eccentric, Duffy's novel nevertheless remains somewhat out in the wilderness, politically speaking; a symptom of green politics' novelty.

Conservation and Conservatism

The charge of political obscurity could not be brought against *Blott on the Landscape* (1975). Tom Sharpe, bestselling satirical writer known for his *Wilt* series (1976–2010), turned his hand to a terrorism novel early in his literary career. Concerning an English country house and broadly conservative in outlook, critics would no doubt challenge the "terrorism" label were it to be applied outside of this comparative study. The subject matter of the novel is more in keeping with the traditions of English farce than Duffy's novel. Where Duffy inverts Englishness, Sharpe celebrates it. The accumulating series of conflicts fit the standard terrorist morphology, however; a riot in a courthouse, the smashing of a village, demolition of a mansion, dynamiting of a gorge and a final, cataclysmic shoot-out with the SAS. The novel features more environmentalist terrorism than even Abbey's *The Monkey Wrench Gang*. The difference, however, lies in the staunchly conservationist and conservative attitudes underlying its P.G. Woodhouse-esque whimsy.

The plot centres around the "vast, rambling building" (2002, 2) of Handyman Hall, ancestral seat of the rambunctious Lady Maud and her scheming husband Sir Giles, MP. Looking to rid himself of the Hall and pocket its value in cash, Sir Giles convinces the Department of Transport to build a motorway from Sheffingham to Knighton. Handyman Hall just happens to be right in the middle of "the ideal route" (2002, 14). By speaking out in Parliament against the proposal, Sir Giles plans to remove any suspicion of foul play while he collects the "compulsory orders and large sums paid in compensation" (2002, 14) for the destruction of his Hall. Lady Maud, proud of the Handyman title and her aristocratic role in local village life, then begins a campaign against the proposed motorway. The family's anglophile handyman Blott (a German war deserter pretending to be Italian to avoid arrest and who is also madly in love with Lady Maud) begins sowing chaos in an attempt to stop the motorway construction. In response to all the resistance the Minister for Transport sends his least competent but most zealous bureaucrat, Dundridge, to lead the construction efforts. Through a labyrinthine narrative of endless plot twists, conspiracies and music hall intrigues, the implacable Dundridge and the intractable Blott escalate their conflict until it becomes a national scandal: "this might be Vietnam or the Lebanon but this is a quiet corner of rural England" (2002, 329). With Dundridge imprisoned and Sir Giles eaten by lions (a zoo is built as one of Lady Maud's many means of defence), the story can triumphantly close with Lady Maud marrying Blott. Blott, in turn, becomes the local, militantly Eurosceptic MP.

Being aristocrats, Sharpe's characters relate to the government in a very different way to other terrorists. Rather than the state appearing as an overwhelmingly powerful force, Sharpe's characterisations (or more accurately caricatures) charge the government with the less insidious crime of incompetency. Dundridge, the chief embodiment of this system, is considered even by his superiors to be "clearly unstable" (2002, 58) and is promoted to higher and higher positions in the hope that he will one day reach a level where direct responsibility will be beneath him and his incompetency won't matter. Dundridge's personal characteristics caricature those of civil servants in general:

> His life had been spent in pursuit of order, an abstract order that would have supplanted the perplexities of experience. As far as he was concerned variety was not the spice of life but gave it a very bitter flavour. In Dundridge's philosophy everything conformed to a norm. On one side there was chance, nature red in tooth and claw and everything haphazard; on the other science, logic and numeration. Dundridge particularly favoured numeration. (2002, 60)

The image of the punctilious civil servant, more interested in rules and regulations than common sense and plain talking, is as much an archetype of the conservative imagination as the fascist policeman is to the radical imagination. Both types stand for the seemingly arbitrary nature of state power. Dundridge, armed with compulsory purchase orders, fuddled London-centric judges and endless reserves of taxpayers' money, makes as devastating a use of the state's monopoly of violence as any police or military official could. Christening the motorway building project "Operation Overland", Dundridge begins "digging up a field here and rooting out a wood there, starting a bridge and then abandoning construction to begin a flyover" (2002, 234). This series of measures he describes as "sorties" into the Handymans' Cleene Gorge constituency. The images of blasted rock, uprooted forests and fleets of giant demolition vehicles recalls the forces of industry and consumerism impinging on Abbey's Wild West, only here they are devastating the landscape on behalf of bland bureaucracy. The land itself, in its flattened desolation, reflects the dry desert of Dundridge's mandarin mindset; the land which has yet to be trampled, torn, and filled with Larkin's "concrete and tires" becomes, by contrast, the last sanctuary of native English fortitude and feeling.

Dundridge's assaults on the environment are a result, Sharpe shows, of his over-logical mindset. This type of character has been a target of British conservative disdain all the way back to Edmund Burke's writings in the late eighteenth century. Reflecting on the French revolution, still only in its earliest stages, Burke foresaw the Terror that would come, attributing it to minds like Dundridge's. "Terrorism", a term originally referring to the policies of Robespierre and the Jacobins, is attributed by Burke to the false power of law overtaking the natural power of tradition. According to Burke, "the people of England well know, that the idea of inheritance assures a principle of conservation, and a sure principle of transmission… our political system is placed in a just correspondence and symmetry with the order of the world" (1986, 119–120). The numeration, science and logic so praised by Dundridge have some inhuman element at its core; one which Burke believes can be rectified only through a deference for experience and common sense. Conservation, whether environmental or in a heritage sense, can be seen as an example of this deference in practice. A respect for the country house and its grounds serves as a bolster against the excesses of government. Expanding the relevance of these principles, Raymond Williams describes how Edmund Burke's anti-revolutionary writings established:

> The idea of what has been called an 'organic society', where the emphasis is on the interrelation and continuity of human activities, rather than on separation into spheres of interest, each governed by its own laws….

immediately after Burke, this complex which he describes was to be called the 'spirit of the nation'; by the end of the nineteenth century, it was to be called a national 'culture'. (1958, 11)

The conservative conservationist attitude and the more radical environmentalist attitude which were in the process of splitting apart during the mid-1970s find an unlikely primogenitor in Burke's writing on the nation. The sense that there is a natural order to society just as there is a natural order to nature may suggest to some a reverence for what is. For others it takes on the radical call to break free of unnatural bonds and return to what, presumably, the state of nature once was. The fears of uncontrolled growth stirred by texts like *The Limits to Growth* and *Blueprint for Survival* explicitly compare industrial disequilibrium with a proposed, alternative, "natural" equilibrium of "a society made up of decentralised, self-sufficient communities, in which people work near their homes [and] have the responsibility of governing themselves" (*The Ecologist* 1972, 62). Interestingly, Lady Maud herself draws upon the language of post-1973 Oil crisis fears, suggesting that the "motorway would be a useless, obsolescent eyesore in fifty years when fossil fuel ran out" (2002, 294). It is thus on the part of nature that the characters of *Blott*... undertake their violent insurrection against the "city-dwellers for whom talk was currency and words were coins" (2002, 321). Against the "unnatural" order which, in a Burkean fashion, is allied to state terrorism, the "natural" insurrectionary violence of the common people becomes not only justified but a social responsibility.

In *Blott on the Landscape*, acts of terrorism directed against the motorway construction are each framed as natural English reactions to the state's imposition on the land. For Ignacio Sanchez-Cuenca, these acts of political violence would therefore no longer be terrorism but guerrilla insurgency:

> [In] the actor-sense of terrorism... terrorism is a political violence carried out by underground organisations that do not control part of the territory of the state in which they act. Guerrilla insurgencies, unlike terrorist organisations, liberate territory, normally in the jungle or the mountains, and rule in the area. (2009, 689)

Perhaps we can then place the Little Englanders of Sharpe's novel beside the guerrillas of the Sierra Maestra or the Viet Cong? With the aid of a shipment of Handyman Triple XXX extra strong special ale, Blott's first insurrectionary action is to incite the townspeople of Cleene Gorge into violent riot against Lord Leakham, a judge sent from London to pronounce upon the motorway in favour of the government.

> It took several baton charges to clear a way through the crowd and all the time the cameras recorded faithfully the public response to the proposed motorway through the Cleene Gorge. In Ferret Lane shop windows were broken. Outside the Goat and Goblet Lord Leakham was drenched with a pail of cold water. In the Abbey Close he was concussed by a portion of broken tombstone, and when he finally reached the Four Feathers the Fire Brigade had to be called to use their hoses to disperse the crowd that besieged the hotel. By that time the Rolls Royce was on fire and drunken youths roamed the streets demonstrating their loyalty to the Handyman family by smashing street lamps. (2002, 55)

The natural home grounds of any truculent English patriot, the country's pubs, are transformed in this passage into a series of outposts for violent insurrectionary activity. The "outside agitation" at the core of the trouble takes the form of the local gentry buying them all a pint. What would under any other circumstances be a form of behaviour deeply condemned and feared by a conservative readership is here rendered comic, if not borderline heroic, by the same discourse of local cultures and decaying traditions Sanchez-Cuenca appeals to in his defence of guerrilla insurgency. Sharpe satirically inverts left-wing apologism for Third-World terrorism by staging his own popular revolution in Little England. Sharpe's revolutionaries rise up in support of rigid social hierarchies and smash the state out of respect for private property (if not public property).

The final showdown between Blott and the government takes place on the exact terms of Burke's conservatism; the primacy of the private over the public, of liberty over legislation. Blott's home, the Lodge, is fortunately situated at the opening to the Handyman estate and provides its only entrance. As Dundridge's wrecking balls and bulldozers approach for their final assault, Blott uses his military skills to barricade himself in, leaving his home, and by extension Handyman Hall, "practically impregnable to anything short of a full-scale assault by tanks and artillery" (2002, 302). Within the Lodge, Blott has amassed "a rifle, a Bren gun, a two-inch mortar, several cases of ammunition and hard-granades" (2002, 303). The lodge itself, we have learned earlier, is "filled with books he had picked up on the market stalls... only books on English history... a scholar's library born of an intense curiosity about the country of his adoption" (2002, 104). After fending off assaults up to and including one by SAS Special Forces, Blott utilises his understanding of the British mindset to attack his own Lodge with the weapons he had amassed, resulting in dramatic news footage. As a result, he becomes a popular underdog hero overnight and Dundridge is arrested. Blott turns his home into a castle, very literally, in order to defend his Lady's ancestral land and, as a result of his success, is made an adoptive Englishman by marriage. Blott's victorious insurgency is a triumph both for the countryside and conservative English values. The relevance of Blott's final speech against the Common Market, forerunner of the European Union, re-emerges here as a way of opposing the "real England" with some foreign, centralising and bureaucratic force. Environmental conservation and nationalist conservatism are united in these final images, allowing Blott's insurgency to take on an anti-establishment character while all along celebrating the values of Britain's ultimate establishment, the aristocracy.

CONSERVATION, COUNTRY HOUSES AND *COUPS D'ETAT*

Concern for the environment took very different shapes on the political left and right in the 1970s. Its shared soil, however, cross-fertilised some dangerous political ideas. Matless, Watkins and Merchant' survey of 1960s conservationism found it surprisingly harmonious, despite considerable ideological differences: "activities which would in future years be presented as in fundamental conflict, such as agriculture and nature conservation, field sports and care for wildlife [were, in the 1960s,] held in balance through a regulatory outlook styling itself as both paternalistic and modern" (2010, 98). The ideological battles of the 1970s were yet to split the movement into radical environmentalism on the one side and conservative conservationism on the other. The cracks where these major fissures would later appear are arguably present from this early point, however. A clear example of such a doomed union being the Conservation Society, the first such society in the U.K., founded in 1966 and growing steadily until the early 1970s when its more radical members left to join Friends of the Earth. The Conservations Society, behind its shared environmentalist cause also shared a belief in the universal provision of contraception. A survey on the question of contraception found that, of its members, "18% described themselves as Conservative, 15% Liberal, 16% Labour, 5% Communist and Left, and 50% were uncommitted" (Herring 2001, 394). The reasoning behind memberships to this broad coalition often totally opposed each other, in spite of their agreement on the policy itself. Political radicals and young urbanites sought birth control as a means to furthering gender equality or else sexual liberation. The conservative branch of the organisation (including Lady Balfour whose Soil Association had strong ties to the British Union of Fascists) pursued the contraception policy with the Malthusian end of population control. The same fear that lies behind left wing versions of ecological dystopias can be traced through the Conservation Society's membership to the "blood and soil" mythologies which gave birth to the organic movement. A fear of an amorphous mob, consuming and breeding, infiltrates much of the discourse of 1970s environmentalism and conservationism, leaving an unpleasant aftertaste to what may otherwise be considered progressive, well intentioned or humanistic causes.

It may be that the tendency toward misanthropy, always prominent at times of economic turmoil, is at least partly responsible for the over-abundance of country houses which appear in conservationist writing. That country house estates should be the focus of the National Trust over and above any other form of historical or heritage site finds its explanation in the view of history again proposed by Burke:

> Why should the expenditure of a great landed property, which is a dispersion of the surplus product of the soil, appear intolerable to you or to me, when it takes its course through the accumulation of vast libraries, which are the history of the force and weakness of the human mind; through great collections of ancient records, medals and coins, which attest and explain laws and customs; though paintings and statues that, by imitating nature, seem to extend the limits of creation? (1986, 272)

Against the Terror in France, Burke sees the country house as quintessentially British. Its age upon age of accumulated wealth is seen to represent an equally impressive accumulation of history, culture and tradition. As long as you ignore the question of who actually owns it, the country house becomes a living symbol of all that is best about Britain, the very essence of Britain itself. Self-contained and orderly, the house must be protected from the rampaging mob out beyond the grounds.

It is in an uncomfortable ideological region somewhere between nostalgia, snobbery, conservationism and misanthropy that the third British terror novel of this chapter, Emma Tennant's *The Last of the Country House Murders* (1974), is located. The narrative is notable for its internal conflict between two terrorisms not usually referred to as terrorisms: the Burkean Terror of an out of control socialist government and the fascist terror of an aristocratic *coup d'etat*. The novel is set in a dystopian future where, following a revolution by the uneducated masses, those aristocrats who did not escape the country are forced to perform their own execution in the form of a televised murder mystery held in their own country house. The last of these aristocrats, Jules Tanner, patiently awaits his execution as the mob surrounds his house with their cameras (the VIP area reserved for "Supplementary Benefit Holders Only" (1974, 57)). He keeps himself entertained by discussing great English poets with the state appointed "detective" Haines. Unlike the punctilious Dundridge, however, Haines is seen to have "a streak of Lucky Jim in him... from his years at Tech" (1974, 18) and starts to become dangerously sympathetic to Jules' stories about his friends Gertrude Stein, Edith Warton and Henry James, as well as the many objects and artworks from an era before "the stately home was no longer England's treasure house" (1974, 62). With the date of the execution nearly at hand, a deus ex machina in the shape of Ayn Randian superman Cedric Brown flies into the rescue:

> Cedric sat at the controls of his white helicopter... It was a long time since he had last left the sanctuary of Princes Point, and what he saw beneath him filled him with horror. Vague stirrings of conscience returned to him at the sight of the crowded tenement towns, over-spills which spilt over into each other in the wild lateral rush for accommodation, the islands of high-rise buildings which stood out like the jaw-bones of prehistoric animals in the despoiled landscape. (1974, 93)

Thankful for the appearance of a superior, "It's Cedric Brown! Up with Cedric! Get us out of this mess, Cedric!" (1974, 97), the mob turn their backs on their revolution and celebrate as Cedric leads an army to seize power from the elected government and reinstate the aristocracy. What begins as the rescue of the sensitive yet stalwart Jules from his death at the hands of a postmodern Robespierre (a rescue in which soldiers heroically "trampled the tourists, suffocated the wedding guests [and] overthrew the coaches in their stampede for freedom and justice" (1974, 158)) soon turns into Cedric rescuing the sprawling unwashed mass of humanity from themselves and installing a military dictatorship.

An heiress to a country house herself, Tennant gives little indication that any of this is intended to be satirical or ironic; the narrative in fact imparts a definite feeling of poorly disguised wish-fulfilment. The novel is unpleasant in its misanthropy, in a way that Sharpe's novel absolutely isn't. From a conservationist opening, Tennant reveals all too clearly that she'd rather conserve things than people.

Yet, as with *The Chilian Club*, there is something compelling in *The Last of the Country House Murders*' extreme and uncensored nature which appeals to the analysis of a divided and divisive 1970s ideological landscape. The constant stream of snobbery when describing the mob, the endless name-dropping by the aristocratic characters which is unfailingly paired with the reminder that Haines, as a functionary, doesn't know who they are referring to, in short the whole style gives the impression of overcompensation. As Francis Wheen has described, the 1970s right wing had a tendency to believe that "flaws in the national character were full and sufficient explanation for the United Kingdom's subsequent decline" (2010, 204). It is this outlook, couched in conservationist politics, that *The Last of the Country House Murders* takes to rather elaborate extremes. The "modern man" is imagined as the antithesis of the country gentleman; the figure for whom the country house was first built. "Inflated by the possession of £300,000 a year," as Mark Girouard describes him, "until all the most admired qualities of his species can be examined over life size" (1979, 4). The desperate libidinal desire for wealth and power from which Thatcherism emerges can be seen to create its own imagined pasts in country houses. The novel's fantasy is of a world where the powerful went unchecked by the impositions of others. Connect this to a nostalgia for heritage sites, the symbolic power of the country estate as embodiment of the nation, and apocalyptic visions of overpopulation and societal collapse, and the resulting tensions begin to manifest themselves in fantastical and violent ways. Where Sharpe and Duffys' novels successfully mediate difficult political sentiments through farce and humour, Tennant's use of comic hyperbole retains a rabid edge which, unpalatable though it can be, perhaps betrays a truer sense of the 1970s' fractious political divides. In this horror-show decade, benign conservationists and allotment gardeners harbour some of the same shattered landscapes, marching jackboots and flying petrol bombs in their political fantasies as one might expect from hardened ideologues.

Notes

1. On the question of terrorism, Abbey dismisses links to his novel which he considers pure fiction, "written to entertain". In an interview (collected in List) he states: "the book does not condone terrorism in any form. Let's have some precision in language here: terrorism means deadly violence—for a political and/or economic purpose—carried out against people and other living things, and is usually conducted by governments against their own citizens" (1993, 252). Abbey plays the definitions game only with his unique definition of "political violence" which, he asserts, refers only to "deadly violence".
2. The name is a reference to William Blake's poem "Auguries of Innocence":
A robin redbreast in a cage
Puts all Heaven in a Rage
Each outcry of the hunted hare
A fibre from the brain does tear. (Duffy 1978, 65)
3. With compulsory National Service having ended only a decade earlier in 1963, the experiences of military discipline would be common to those of Duffy's generation. Duffy's close friend and fellow author B.S. Johnson edited a collection, *All Bull* (1973), in the same year as *IWTGTM*, recounting tales of routine bullying and mistreatment during peacetime conscription.

Bibliography

Abbey, Edward. 1975. *The Monkey Wrench Gang*. New York: Avon Books.
———. 1993. Earth First! and the Monkey Wrench Gang. In *Radical Environmentalism: Philosophy and Tactics*, ed. Peter C. List. Belmont: Wadsworth Publishing.
Burke, Edmund. 1986. *Reflections on the Revolution in France*. London: Penguin.
———. 2008. *A Philosophical Enquiry into the Origins of Our Ideas of the Sublime and the Beautiful*. Oxford: Oxford Classics.
Butler, Andrew M. 2012. *Solar Flares: Science Fiction in the 1970s*. Liverpool: Liverpool University Press.
Carson, Rachel. 1965. *Silent Spring*. London: Penguin.
Chisholm, Michael. 1974. Regional Policies for the 1970s: The Eva G. R. Taylor Memorial Lecture, 1973. *The Geographical Journal* 140 (2): 215–231.
Doherty, Brian, Matthew Paterson, and Benjamin Steel (eds.). 2000. *Direct Action in British Environmentalism*. London: Routledge.
Duffy, Maureen. 1978. *I Want to Go to Moscow*. London: Penguin.

Gay, Hannah. 2012. Before and After *Silent Spring*: From Chemical Pesticides to Biological Control and Integrated Pest Management—Britain, 1945–1980. *Ambix* 59 (2): 88–108.
Girouard, Mark. 1979. *The Victorian Country House*. New Haven: Yale University Press.
Herring, Horace. 2001. The Conservation Society: Harbinger of the 1970s Environment Movement in the U.K. *Environment and History* 7 (4): 381–401.
Ikenberry, G. John. 1986. The Irony of State Strength: Comparative Responses to the Oil Shocks of the 1970s. *International Organization* 40 (1): 105–137.
Jorgensen, Dolly. 2012. A Blueprint for Destruction: Eco-Activism in *Doctor Who* During the 1970s. *Ecozon@: European Journal of Literature, Culture and Environment* 3 (2): 11–26.
Larkin, Philip. 1972. Prologue. In *How Do You Want to Live? A Report on the Human Habitat*. London: Department of the Environment.
———. 1974. Going, Going. In *High Windows*. London: Faber and Faber.
Lessing, Doris. 1998. *Walking in the Shade: Volume Two of My Autobiography, 1949–1962*. London: Flamingo.
List, Peter C. 1993. *Radical Environmentalism: Philosophy and Tactics*. Belmont: Wadsworth Publishing.
Marwick, Arthur. 1998. *The Sixties*. Oxford: Oxford University Press.
Matless, David, Charles Watkins, and Paul Merchant. 2010. Nature Trails: The Production of Instructive Landscapes in Britain, 1960–72. *Rural History* 21 (1): 97–131.
McKay, George. 2011. *Radical Gardening: Politics, Idealism and Rebellion in the Garden*. London: Frances Lincoln.
Meadows, Donella H., Dennis L. Meadows, Jorgen Randers, and William W. Behrens III. 1972. *The Limits to Growth: A Report for the Club of Rome's Project on the Predicament of Mankind*. London: Earth Island Books.
Moorcock, Michael. 1976. *The Adventures of Una Persson and Catherine Cornelius in the Twentieth Century*. London: Granada.
Pedler, Kit, and Gerry Davis. 1975. *The Dynostar Menace*. London: Pan.
Rawcliffe, Peter. 1998. *Environmental Pressure Groups in Transition*. Manchester: Manchester University Press.
Rodwell, Dennis. 2010. Urban Conservation in the 1970s and 1970s: A European Overview. *Architectural Heritage* 21 (1): 1–18.
Sanchez-Cuenca, Ignacio. 2009. Revolutionary Dreams and Terrorist Violence in the Developed World: Explaining Country Variation. *Journal of Peace Research* 46 (5): 687–705.
Sharpe, Tom. 2002. *Blott on the Landscape*. London: Arrow.

Tennant, Emma. 1974. *The Last of the Country House Murders*. London: Faber and Faber.
The Ecologist. 1972. *A Blueprint for Survival*. London: Penguin.
Wheen, Francis. 2010. *Strange Days Indeed*. London: Fourth Estate.
Williams, Raymond. 1958. *Culture and Society*. London: The Hogarth Press.

CHAPTER 7

Conclusion

> Who are these inhuman bombers that strike... at the very heart of our society with no respect for human life, without even the courtesy of a perfunctory warning? It makes you nostalgic, doesn't it, for the good old days of the IRA. 'Cause they gave warnings, didn't they? They were gentleman bombers... decent British terrorists. They didn't want to be British. But they were. (Lee 2010, 178)

Stewart Lee's joke, made during his 2006 tour '*90s Comedian*, was delivered against a background of intense paranoia regarding Islamic terrorism. It sets up a distinction, in Lee's arch and ironic style, between the clarity of the IRA's motives against the seemingly incomprehensible reasons behind Al Qaida's jihad. The routine is transcribed in Lee's book *How I Escaped My Certain Fate* (2010) with a footnote describing how the IRA were referred to as "gentleman bombers" in routines by two other comedians, Patrick Kielty and Andrew Maxwell, in two different routines created simultaneous to his own in 2005. The target of all three jokes, he argues, was the Western media portrayal of "Islamic terrorists as motiveless fundamentalist psychopaths, as opposed to the more finely nuanced forms of terrorism and terrorists we have here in the civilised world" (2010, 178). Lee's critique was and remains common among liberals in Britain; the sense that terrorism takes many forms and Al Qaida is only prominent on the news due to Western racism. By ironically praising the IRA for their "British values," Lee shows up British reaction: insular when faced with external threats and nostalgic when faced with new ones.

Arguably, this joke wouldn't work at all if Lee's audience were actually nostalgic about the IRA. The joke depends upon Lee's mastery of persona and his ability to deliver a line while communicating to the audience that he really believes the opposite. It is funny precisely because the IRA have not been forgiven by the majority of the British public but they, through the strange workings of history, have taken on a more benign appearance in contrast with the likes of Al Qaida. There are still many unresolved and complex feelings surrounding the conflict in Northern Ireland. The work of the Peace Process continues and with every step forward there are living traumas and unresolved injustices which have to be engaged with. On the British mainland too there is an increasing need to understand this conflict in a way that previous generations haven't. I was lucky enough during my time at the University of Salford to work alongside Professor Scott Brewster and Dr. Caroline Magennis on an English literature programme which included a whole module about the conflict. Literature's ability to allow readers to see past media shorthand and engage with the lived realities of the conflict is promising, as is the considerable numbers of students that these modules attract every year.

Of particular interest in terms of the British involvement in the Northern Irish conflict is the film *'71*, released in the UK in 2014 and directed by Yann Demange. In contrast to *Harry's Game* which used its undercover protagonist to present what is essentially an Irish conflict, *'71* instead constructs a panoramic vision of Belfast's combatants in the year of its title. The protagonist Garry Hook, played by Jack O'Connell, is a working class British soldier who we are introduced to as he trains with his squadron on the Yorkshire moors. He is likable and naive, joining the army to serve his country. Once he is shipped out to Belfast it is clear that he is out of his depth and under siege. We only see him leave the barracks in order to patrol and on each patrol he is met with screaming locals, thrown stones and, eventually, IRA snipers. At this point in the film the audience feels immersed in the British experience of the conflict—lost, confused and under threat—which swiftly turns to panic as Garry is separated from his unit and lost in the winding backstreets of Belfast. It is here where the movie switches perspective and we are presented with the complex array of competing forces all with an interest in Hook's conundrum. We are shown the conflict between Official IRA characters who want to keep out of the situation and the young Provisionals who want to capture the soldier. Within the Provisionals, however, there is also conflict between older members with political experience and younger, wilder members who would rather kill the soldier than capture him. All of these forces are themselves tied up in complex networks of subterfuge, as are the family of unaligned Catholics who eventually take Garry in. The British rescue forces are in a state of internal conflict too; the army rescue effort, led by Lieutenant Armitage, are constantly delayed by the MRF's Captain Browning who, playing all sides against each other, seeks to use Hook as a bartering tool between the many competing IRA factions. The conflict in Belfast is portrayed as a brutal mess of labyrinthine complexity. There is no attempt at an ideological explanation of the issues behind the conflict, certainly no religious ones, it is instead presented as complex and cruel; a space where no moral or ideological standpoint could enter without being compromised. One might criticise the film for this choice. However, as a film which seeks to explore a historical moment when memories are still raw, *'71* offers a working through of the conflict on a human level. All the characters (other than the wild youths) are comprehensible in their actions. Their moral decisions are not personal but emerge from the circumstances of the conflict itself. As a film released in 2014, *'71* may represent an increased curiosity on the part of British audiences to return to the conflict as part of our own history, as well as the history of peoples across the Irish Sea.

A less subtle process of revisitation appears to have taken place around left-wing urban guerrillas. Julian Preece's study *Baader-Meinhof and the Novel* (2012) traces the history of Red Army Faction fiction from a brief spike of interest in the 1970s (equivalent to the British response to The Angry Brigade) through a more reflective 1980s and 1990s, until a new wave of interest picked up in the years after 2001. Beginning as an ironic take on the Che Guevara t-shirts and Mao buttons of the 1970s, a "Prada Meinhof" craze threatened to go mainstream in the late 1990s. Matt Worley of *The Guardian*'s fashion section celebrated how "come the revolution, we'll all be in combats" (1999). I have even heard talk of an actual Prada fashion line that was cancelled after 9/11 but have yet to find evidence of it. Either way, the trend continued and perhaps even gained momentum in the early 2000s with the film *The Baader-Meinhof Complex* (2008) winning the Oscar for Best Foreign Language Film and a number of German novels being published with Red Army Faction protagonists including Thilo Bock's *The Loaded Shooter of Andreas Baader* (2009), Thomas Weiss' *Death of a Truffle Pig* (2007) and Ulrich Peltzer's *Part of the Solution* (2007). As Preece writes, "the cause of the political action each time is globalised capitalism and its effects on German society" (2012, 147). The suggestion is that the Red Army Faction, largely shorn of their terroristical edge, are recuperated as anti-capitalist heroes and all purpose rebels. Their contrived ultra-left positions (aligning Israel with Nazism, for example) bear an increasing relation to mainstream leftist theory after the fall of communism. Reinforced by the belief that terrorism is a construct exaggerated by the media, Red Army Faction apologists adopt the terrorist group as ironic, taboo, retro figureheads of resistance.

It was in fact a British novel about the Red Army Faction, Ada Wilson's *Red Army Faction Blues* (2012), which inspired the writing of this book. I had been reading terrorist novels in my spare time for two years at that point and, alongside teaching and research responsibilities, I had also become highly involved with the students' movement against tuition fees. Manchester's student movement had, since 2010, centred around the occupation of the Roscoe building at the University of Manchester. Like a true radical I had been the third through the door when the building was initially taken. Like a true Mancunian I then left to go to the pub once things stopped being exciting. In those student pubs—Jabez Clegg, The Thirsty Scholar, The Sand Bar, The Crescent— Route Publishing had had the brilliant idea of putting beer mats printed with adverts for their forthcoming novel. The beer mats read, in black lettering, "A coalition government. A widely mistrusted ruling elite. Riots in the streets and heavy-handed police tactics," and then following this, in red, "Welcome to West Berlin, 1967" (2012). The parallels to our own situation were immediately obvious. I immediately arranged to receive a review copy. The novel is in fact a rumination on left wing radicalism before and after the fall of the Berlin Wall, set between 1967 and 1989, but the 1970s references points, including a search for Fleetwood Mac's original frontman Peter Green, lend the book a definitively 1970s feel. It tied perfectly into the protester's desire to see themselves reliving revolutionary history. Like the Parisians of 1848 dressing as the Parisians of 1789, history was happening "first as tragedy, then as farce" (Marx 2001, 329). A book on the 1970s was consciously marketed as a book about 2010. We had entered the era of terrorism as farce, something we had perhaps been prepared for by the hundreds of comedians laughing at Al Qaida, or sly references to the IRA being obsolete, or the sense that the world had indeed changed and, after the Blair years, we were all liberals now, racists and fascists being only a tiny minority of buffoons.

There is something about the recuperation of urban guerrillas among the radical left which speaks to a fundamental lack of seriousness about real change. Terrorist acts in 1970s British novels are already framed as acts demonstrating a superior will; a radical performance of one's beliefs that makes their commitment palpable in a physical, undeniable way. When, at the last moment, the protagonist fails to see through their last big operation then their beliefs often fail with them; as if such beliefs could not be maintained without being acted upon. These beliefs are not sustainable in the real world and can exist only in opposition. I think we all have these kinds of beliefs within us. The threat comes when circumstances conspire to bring together individuals with anti-social beliefs and then provoke them with an escalating series of conflicts.

So, what are the differences between terrorism now and terrorism then? To return to Al Qaida, and Islamic terror more generally, a direct comparison can be found in Anthony Burgess' *1985* (1978). Written to mark the thirtieth anniversary of *1984*, the book is separated into critical analysis of Orwell's text in the first half and a novella by Burgess in the second. After writing an average of two novels a year in the 1960s, Burgess spent most of the 1970s working on his epic *Earthly Powers* (1980). According to Andrew Biswell, the process of writing a long novel depressed Burgess so much that his wife secretly organised for publishers Little, Brown & Company to commission *1985* (xii). The break from *Earthly Powers* must have worked as the long novel came out two years later. That the writing of this book was a holiday from a longer, more serious work, perhaps excuses the occasionally unpolished nature of Burgess' response to Orwell.

1985 ostensibly aims to predict what the year 1984 would actually be like, although from the start Burgess makes his case that good science fiction says more about the present than the future. In his analysis of *1984* Burgess makes much of Orwell's borrowings from 1940s London life: Airstrip One is shown to include bombed-out terraces, Victory cigarettes, and a moustachioed Big Brother who looked suspiciously like the man in the Bennett College ads (tagline: "let me be your big brother" (Burgess 2016, 11)). Burgess' version of 1984 is, as a result, an exaggerated 1978. The trade unions initiate general strikes every other day, multiracial gangs run the streets, the government is powerless, pornography is shown on daytime TV and strike breaking is punished by court-mandated sensitivity training. The story follows Bev Jones, a confectioner whose wife is burned to death during a fire service strike. Following a Christmas day without power (rolling blackouts are a recurring motif), Bev decides to go "antistate" (2016, 120). He joins a gang of literati street thugs, burns his union card and turns up to work during a strike. The last offense is enough to land him in the "Trade Union Congress Education Centre" (2016, 158) where he must face down the softly spoken syndicalist professor Mr Pettigrew; a version of Orwell's O'Brien who, instead of torture, wins over his audience with affability and homely arguments (he is perhaps modelled on Tony Benn). So far, so 1970s.

The relevance for our current study comes with the introduction of the Free Britons. Seemingly a fascist organisation opposing syndicalism with nationalism, their propaganda makes passing reference to "the God of the prophets, from Abraham to Mohamed" (2016, 132). "Now can you see where the money's coming from?" (2016, 132) Bev is asked, upon noticing this phrase. The Free Britons are revealed to be a private army funded by "Pan-Islamic" (2016, 177) oil money aiming to restore order through Islam. As their leader, Colonel Lawrence, argues "the only way out of Britain's troubles… is a return to responsibility, loyalty, religion. A return to God. And who will show us that God now? The Christians? Christianity was abolished by the second Vatican council" (2016, 179). The final showdown of the novel takes place when workers building a London Mosque refuse to stop work during a general strike. They are attacked by trade unionists who are in turn attacked by the Free Britons. In the ensuing carnage Burgess makes clear that both sides are as bad as each other: the syndicalists denounce the Islamist "blacklegs", the Islamists denounce the syndicalist "infidels" (2016, 176). Burgess' version of 1984 is a world without a moral centre. For Catholic Burgess, the second Vatican council marks the end of the West's religious superiority as surely as the 1973 Oil Crisis marks the end of its economic superiority. The centre has been hollowed out and in its place are partial interests. The totalising narratives of syndicalism and Islam are presented as incapable of mutual communication. There is, for Burgess, no common ground, with even high culture (usually a great force for moral improvement within his writings) being reduced to a kind of anti-social counterculture kept alive by street gangs.

In spite of its tabloid qualities (Burgess lived in Italy when he wrote the novel and only knew Britain through news reports (Biswell 2016, xii)), *1985* makes a valuable contribution to our understanding of ideologies and terror. Where Orwell's novel warns against tyrannies of the Hitlerian and Stalinist type, Burgess realises that totalitarian government is only one threat and, by the 1970s, an unlikely one (2016, 50). Total domination of thought is unlikely to last, Burgess argues, rather "there is a lot of power about, and its [dangers are] not centralised" (2016, 55). By presenting a Britain dominated by syndicalism, *1985* demonstrates how a political philosophy can devastate a country without even controlling the government. Once all the trade unions align there is no power left for the government other than to sign off on worker's pay rises. Under syndicalism the unions control every part of society without even being in charge: head teachers bow to teachers' union demands, police chiefs bow to police union demands, and if the government makes laws that the unions disagree with then general strikes will assure that those laws are repealed. The importance of this insight on the symbolic level is that it demonstrates how ideologies can be dangerous without having official power. The world presented in *1985* is a gross exaggeration of the real 1970s, but in that excess it captures the feeling of intransigence and decay typical of the era. An era needn't be dominated by a single bad ideology for individuals to lose their freedom.

Our own times have been ravaged by ideologies, but, again, not in the same way that Burgess predicted. It is worth noting that the Free Britons in *1985* are not terrorists. They present themselves as a fascist party, harbour a secret mission to Islamicise Britain, and operate as a paramilitary force defending Arab property. These operations more closely resemble Wahhabi organisations than terrorist groups like Al Qaida, ISIS or Al Shabaab. Indeed, Wahhabism takes both an Orwellian/*1984* form within the Gulf states themselves and a Burgessian/*1985* form across the wider Middle East where its influence is cultural, not governmental. What Islamist terrorism represents, however, is the next step in the dialectic. In spite of ties to Saudi Arabia, Al Qaida do not represent a linear continuation of Wahhabi soft power, rather they are a case of an ideology breaking away from its natural environment and having unexpected, self-destructive results. If we were to posit our own *1986* I would suggest that this would be our main antagonist. Where Burgess demonstrated that ideologists can damage a society with or without the state's approval, modern terror demonstrates how ideologies can damage a society with or without the approval of the ideologists who first expounded them. It is no good saying that the Islamic State is not Islamic when their extremism lies in taking the rhetoric of Islamist preachers seriously. We see the same in Charlottesville, and in the Yemen, and in Turkey. It lingers in Antifa and in the next generation of Northern Irish militants. Everywhere there are young people whose extremism amounts to taking seriously the things that their elders have said.

Which returns us to the British terrorist novels of the 1970s. What these novels dare to say is that there is usually something at the core of a terrorist's mission which a conscientious person could sympathise with. We would all like an end to exploitation, to imperialism, to discrimination, and we'd all like a fairer society, and to treat animals better, and to save the environment. The protagonists of these novels are sympathetic for these reasons. The terrorist morphology demonstrates how the journey from these beliefs to terrorism is one that, equally, might happen to any of us should we be convinced enough in our beliefs or unlucky enough in our encounters with authority. But terrorists can also be caricatures in these novels, and monsters. Some are irredeemable. Some are just evil. I don't like trite lessons, but I think we can learn from both of these depictions. We shouldn't be afraid of culture that tries to understand terrorism, nor should we be suspicious of culture which condemns it. For the modern reader's taste, writers from the 1970s can appear shameless in the things they say. By contrast, our writers today must struggle not be shamed into silence. It might be that we must look back to see forward.

Bibliography

Biswell, Andrew. 2016. Introduction. In *1985*, Anthony Burgess (author). London: Serpent's Tail.
Burgess, Anthony. 2016. *1985*. London: Serpent's Tail.
Demange, Yann (Dir.). (2014). *'71*. Crab Apple Films.
Lee, Stewart. 2010. *How I Escaped My Certain Fate*. London: Faber and Faber.
Marx, Karl. 2001. The Eighteenth Brumaire of Louis Bonaparte. In *Karl Marx: Selected Writings*, ed. David McLellan, 329–355.
Preece, Julian. 2012. *Baader-Meinhof and the Novel*. London: Palgrave Macmillan.
Wilson, Ada. 2012. *Red Army Faction Blues*. Pontefract: Route.
Worley, Matt. 1999. Come the Revolution, We'll All Be in Combats. *The Guardian*. Web. https://www.theguardian.com/lifeandstyle/1999/nov/19/fashion3. Accessed 19 Nov 1999.

INDEX

A
Abbey, Edward, 6, 84, 123, 124, 126, 129, 130, 132, 134, 139
Al Qaida, 1, 27, 68, 143, 144, 146, 147, 149
Ambler, Eric, 4, 35, 45, 46, 56
Aristocracy, 6, 48, 73, 74, 131, 135, 137, 138

B
Blanqui, Louis Auguste, 12, 13, 16
Bloody Sunday, 62–65, 67, 72
A Blueprint for Survival, 121
Burgess, Anthony, 6, 37, 98, 147–149
Burke, Edmund, 11, 12, 122, 132, 134, 136
Burns, Alan, 5, 103–106, 108, 109, 111

C
Carter, Angela, 5, 102
Chesterton, G.K., 12
Cold War, 27, 28, 34, 42

Common Market, 49, 135
Communist Party, 20, 51, 79, 104
Conrad, Joseph, 12, 40, 53

D
Davies, Jack, 5, 113
Davis, Gerry, 6, 119
Duffy, Maureen, 6, 124, 125, 127, 128, 130, 138, 139

F
Fascism, 15, 20, 50, 52, 54, 88, 102, 111, 131, 137, 147–149
Forsyth, Fredrick, 4, 34, 47, 48, 56
French revolution, 11, 132

G
Guevara, Ernesto "Che", 9, 16, 17, 63, 88, 92, 114, 145
Greene, Graham, 4, 16, 33, 36–41, 43, 45, 46, 54, 84

H
Happening, 90, 99, 109, 126, 146
Ho Chi Minh, 19, 37, 88

J
Johnson, B.S., 5, 103, 106, 109–112, 114, 139

L
Larkin, Philip, 117, 118, 122, 132
Lessing, Doris, 5, 79–81, 83, 125
The Limits to Growth, 121, 133

M
Marighella, Carlos, 18, 63, 72, 112, 114
Marxism, 3, 38
Moorcock, Michael, 6, 119

N
Naipaul, V.S., 4, 16, 33, 41, 43, 45, 46, 54, 84
Nazi, 3, 15, 146
Nuttall, Jeff, 5, 87, 89–92, 98–104, 109, 114

O
Oil crisis, 4, 28, 45, 50, 120, 133, 148

P
Palestine, 10, 15, 16, 20, 34, 35, 44–46, 55, 70, 83, 88
Pedler, Kit, 6
Post-structuralism, 9
Post-war consensus, 29, 88, 120

R
Robespierre, Maximilien, 11, 14, 25, 132, 137

S
Seymour, Gerald, 5, 59, 65–70, 72, 83, 84
Sharpe, Tom, 6, 124, 130–134, 138
Shipway, George, 4, 50, 53
Sorel, George, 15, 17, 94, 97, 111
Soviet Union, 5, 20, 28, 34, 51, 79, 82, 104
Standard terrorist morphology, 29, 30, 47, 51, 80, 106, 123, 130
Sterling, Claire, 5, 20, 28, 34, 35, 51, 56, 78, 79, 82

T
Tennant, Emma, 6, 124, 137, 138
Theroux, Paul, 5, 74, 78
Third World, 28, 35, 41, 42, 92, 93
Trocchi, Alexander, 90, 98, 100, 101
Tse-tung, Mao, 16, 17

U
Underground press, 21, 76, 91, 95, 96, 101, 106, 120

V
Vietnam, 19, 20, 84, 101, 123, 131, 133

W
Williams, Raymond, 4, 50, 53, 96, 132
Wilson, A.N., 5, 73, 74
Wise, Arthur, 4, 50, 52–54

The manufacturer's authorised representative in the EU is Springer Nature Customer Service Centre GmbH, Europaplatz 3, 69115 Heidelberg, Germany. If you have any concerns regarding our products, please contact ProductSafety@springernature.com

Printed and bound by CPI Group (UK) Ltd, Croydon, CR0 4YY
23/03/2026
02076459-0009